I Am Enough

A Journey of Self-Love and Self-Acceptance

Based on a true story

Kamini Naicker

I Am Enough
A Journey of Self-Love and Self-Acceptance
Kamini Naicker

ISBN (paperback): 978-1-7391003-0-8
ISBN (e-book): 978-1-7391003-1-5

Photography: Emil Wessels
Cover design and book layout: Susan Veach
Book manager: Kathryn Bartman

Contents

CHAPTER 1
Armour of Faith

It was late September 2003 that it was arranged for Kate to go on a blind date by a friend of her aunt's, Jane. She would often visit at Kate's family home over the weekends and wondered why Kate was not seeing anyone. Jane worked with Dick and had shown him a photo of Kate, and he was keen to meet Kate in person.

Kate was a very shy person and was quite content with being single at this stage of her life. She was focused on achieving good grades and completing her pharmacy degree the following year. Most people would describe Kate as having the perfect figure, not too tall and not too short or 1,64 meters to be exact. Kate's hair was highlighted with a bronzed tint and when blow waved, the layers fell softly just over her shoulders. Her most striking physical features would be her beautiful smile, immaculate feet and shapely behind.

In exchange, Kate had asked for a photo of Dick. Jane believed that Dick was the perfect person for her—very homely, highly successful, funny and good looking. Kate had not dated anyone for almost two years and was still heartbroken from her first relationship and the breakup. Dick looked cute in the photo, and so she happily agreed to meet him.

Kate and Dick met on a Sunday afternoon at a coffee shop in a shopping mall. Kate had a sense of calm about her as she stood by the elevator waiting for Dick. A very skinny frame approached her, and her initial thought was *is this the same person in the photo?* Dick shook her hand, and they introduced themselves and made their way to the coffee shop. There was no initial attraction or interest in Dick. On the contrary, Dick was very engaged and showed interest in Kate. She did not feel drawn to him, nor did she enjoy much of the conversation. At the time, *South African Idols* was on television, and Kate opted to use this as a reason to leave early. Dick teased her about this as she lived ten minutes away from the shopping mall, and there was plenty of time before the show aired.

In days to follow, Kate received emails and phone calls from Dick, and he persisted in asking her out on a second date. During this time, Kate was writing final exams in the third year of her pharmacy degree. After a stressful day at the university, Kate agreed to a second date. Dick was to fetch her from home and meet her parents. Dick arrived in his work attire and was wearing reading glasses. Kate's dad was the typical proud father as he asked Dick outright, who he was, what he did and where he worked. The silence was awkward and, not long after, the brief introductions ended with her dad asking where they were going, and stating that Kate had to return home by 22:00 at the latest! Kate was surprised as she had never been given a curfew before.

The intention was to have dinner, but Kate and Dick both ended up having desserts for the time that they were out. The evening was filled with much laughter and enjoyable conversation. After a wonderful evening, Kate was receptive to perhaps a potential relationship being established with friendship forming the basis. Perhaps it was not necessary to have the initial attraction.

On the 17th October 2003, Dick asked Kate out to lunch. After lunch as he walked her back to her car, he took out a letter which he read to her, describing his initial feelings for her, and proceeded to officially ask Kate to be his girlfriend. Kate thought it was sweet, and so she agreed!

In the weeks to come, Kate met Dick's immediate family, his mother, elder brother and younger sister. On the first day that Kate met his family, Dick drove extensively to accommodate family commitments and spend time with her.

Dick lived in the South of Johannesburg, and Kate lived in the North of Johannesburg, which meant it was at least a forty-five-minute drive to see each other. Kate was pleased with Dick's commitment and effort in wanting to spend quality time with her.

On the 23rd November 2003, Kate turned 21. In the months leading up to her birthday, Kate convinced her dad that she was not going to ever get married and requested that he throw her a big 21st party instead! Kate was of course unaware in preparation for her birthday bash that she was going to meet Dick two months prior to her birthday.

Going into her 21st birthday, Kate was a noticeably confident university student that was content with life. Her former years were filled with a passion for cricket and photography and, as a result, she had made a few friends at the store at which she printed out her photos. There was a guy at the photo store that was always super eager and enthusiastic to assist Kate when she walked into the shop. He agreed to be her photographer, and so she went ahead and set up a photo shoot to be done at home. Kate had an idea that the invite for her party would also serve as a gift for family and friends to take away. She created a CD that contained all her favourite song tracks at the time. Her favourite picture from the photoshoot was used as the cover of the album that she created.

Kate's birthday fell on a Sunday. On the morning of her birthday, Dick arrived with a big bunch of red roses and white lilies. She also received a frame with a sketch entitled *Armour of Faith* with a message on the back which read as follows:

"Moments will exist when we are apart
moments will exist when you miss me
moments will exist when you forget me
moments will exist when you feel scared
moments will exist when you wonder,
'Does he feel the same as I do for him?'
in those moments there is, more than ever,
an invisible Armour of Faith that holds you

> in love, this armour, created from love,
> love for you, a love that is as strong as
> your love for me, in every single way,
> an indestructible, impenetrable, secure
> suit of armour, for which you are the only host,
> because you are the 'one' no other can fit it,
> because no other deserves it more than you,
> so, when these moments exist, remember
> that his love is an Armour of Faith
> that will never fade or disintegrate,
> that will never submit to external forces
> that can only be broken by the bearer,
> you have created this armour and it will
> be there for as long as you want it,
> for as long as you love and cherish it!
> I LOVE YOU
> HAPPY 21st BIRTHDAY"

Kate had never had someone write such deep and special words before. The words were overwhelming to a degree. She could not believe that there was someone that was highly committed to building a relationship with her. Could she trust this? Was this real?

Kate was invited out for breakfast by Dick, and her best friend from the university joined them as well. This was followed by a special home-cooked meal prepared by her mum which consisted of the most amazing spread and Kate's favourites! Kate's mum is an incredible cook and baker and no matter what she made, it always turned out delectable. The evening was followed by yet another surprise planned by Dick. Kate had expensive taste, and she cheekily would make subtle hints to Dick to test the waters and see just how committed he was to win her over. Kate was already dressed for the occasion in her bottle green, figure-hugging, just over the knee-length dress which was complemented by an elegant pair of strappy black high heel sandals. Kate was intrigued by what the evening might hold, and her mind began to wonder as they began the drive to the special surprise! Dick was driving toward the direction of her university, and the only place she could think of out in that direction was the luxurious hotel that was perched at the top of a hill and overlooked Johannesburg. It was a beautiful hotel with the most magnificent views of the city! Kate's wishes had been granted, and they shortly drove into the grounds of the Westcliff Hotel in Johannesburg. Kate was completely blown away and extremely delighted to be dined by Dick in a romantic five-star restaurant. The three-course meal was delicious, and the ambience impressive as the musicians serenaded Kate and later sang "Happy Birthday" to her. The final course of the evening was a personalised chocolate ganache cake, and her birthday gift from Dick. Kate could not wait to open the small, gift-wrapped box.

As she unwrapped the paper, she could not help but blush and feel extremely shy as Dick watched her unwrapping the gift. Kate's gift was a promise ring. A promise ring is a symbol of a pre-engagement commitment to a monogamous relationship. Kate was totally blown away, and in high spirits. But what exactly did this promise ring mean? Kate was extremely naïve and did not know where this was headed.

Kate's 21st party took place on the Friday evening after her birthday. Dick stayed with her dad at the venue to complete the set-up and ensure that all was in place before returning home to get showered and ready for the party. It warmed Kate's heart to know that Dick was now getting along with her dad. This was the first time that the two most important men of her life were spending time alone together. On their way home, Kate's dad mentioned to Dick that she had extremely expensive taste and was accustomed to high standards when it came to choices or preferences in life. Her dad had worked very hard and done his utmost to ensure that Kate had the perfect launchpad for her future.

Kate was on an absolute high; she was getting ready to enjoy an evening spent with her family and closest friends celebrating, and boy did Kate's family know how to have a good party! Kate picked out a two-piece, deep red wine, flowing outfit that accentuated her figure. The top crossed over in the middle with many gathers and elegantly sat slightly off each shoulder and extended to just above her belly button. The waist band on the pants similarly had many gathers which crossed over in the midline and flowed downwards, with two slits on each leg. Kate looked absolutely stunning and was most certainly the lady in red for the evening. As a result of this sassy outfit, it was decided the week before that Kate would arrive at her party in a fire engine!

In the months leading up to her birthday, Kate had gone for dance lessons with her dad and they had practised the fox trot with which they would open the dance floor that evening. Kate was not joking when she said she was not getting married, and so she wanted to have the first dance with her dad, her protector and provider. Kate's brother- in-law was extremely kind and decided to include Dick in the family formalities and invited Dick to say a few words. The gesture caught Dick off-guard, and it was very out of character for him to be at a sudden loss for words. Fortunately, he had Jane assisting him in the audience as he explained to everyone that he had known Kate for just over two months. Kate's family and friends were captivated by Dick and interested to see the new budding romance between the young couple blossom. It was an awesome celebration filled with lots of laughter, dancing and happy memories. Priceless photos were captured from the evening and clearly depicted Dick's deep infatuation with Kate.

In the weeks to come, the excitement and thrill dissipated as reality kicked in. Dick was not allowed to see Kate during the week, as he needed to go home to have dinner with his family each evening. Dick would see Kate on a Friday and Saturday evening, and Sunday lunches were again set aside for Dick to spend time with his family. It was an exceedingly difficult concept for Kate to understand why Dick's mom would insist that a grown man would be required to spend so much time at home whilst he was in a committed courtship with the intention to marry. Prior to meeting Kate, Dick spent most of his time at home playing computer games and being there for his mom and sister. Dick's parents divorced when he was in grade eleven. At the time, his elder brother had just gotten married, and so Dick assumed the father figure role in their household.

Dick and Kate had many arguments and fights about the way his time was split. Kate had to live with the fact that a great amount of time was still to be dedicated to his family although they were newly in love, and she was wanting to spend more time with him. It felt like a continuous tug of war for Kate. Whenever Kate mentioned the yearning for his time, Dick would support his mother's view and explain that he was always there for his mother and sister, and that they were struggling to adapt with Kate being around.

CHAPTER 2
The Outlaws

In December 2003, Dick and his family were going on a summer holiday to Cape Town. Both his brother's girlfriend and Kate were invited to join, but the girls ended up not going and remained in Johannesburg. Again, it was a difficult period for Kate as Dick could not speak much to her over the phone since he was preoccupied with his family both during the day and in the evenings. When Kate compared this to her first relationship, she did not experience any of this and was not accustomed to being second priority after a guy's family! Kate was a mature young lady and understood that this was Dick's family and time still needed to be spent with them; however, the honeymoon phase of the relationship came to a quick halt following Kate's birthday. Kate was longing to get to know Dick better and spend more time with him, but first she needed to get through his mother and sister!

Dick was highly successful at a very young age, and all due to his own strength and drive. Dick's parents got divorced when he was in his second last year of secondary school. They got back together for a brief period whilst his brother got married for the first time, and then finally split again. Dick was the middle child and most definitely his mother's favourite; yet on the contrary, he was very independent and instrumental in his own success. Kate had always been extremely proud of his career successes and how quickly he climbed up the corporate ladder.

Dick returned from Cape Town just prior to New Year's Eve. He bought Kate a special gift that was an intricate sculpture of a boy and girl with angel wings on their backs, standing on a tree branch kissing each other through a vine adorned with flowers. The gift most certainly made up for the lonely preceding two weeks!

Within three months of Kate and Dick meeting, he returned home one day and shared with his mother and sister that Kate was the woman of his dreams. He wanted to marry her, and she was to be the mother of his children one day. Prior to this, Dick only had one meaningful relationship which lasted a full three months. Based on this, you can only imagine how the news brought additional insecurity and anxiety to Dick's mother and sister. How was it possible that he had decided this early into the relationship that Kate was the one?!

The initial meeting with Dick's family was fine. Although Kate felt very shy and self-conscious, Dick's family seemed nice enough. The relationship between Kate and Dick's mother and sister became estranged as the continuous disagreement on how Dick split his time between his family and Kate became an issue. Kate was constantly fighting an uphill battle, and Dick just would not stand his ground when it came to his family.

Moreover, Dick was the only guy that Kate had met that still had friendships with previous ex-girlfriends. This made Kate feel awkward, as she believed that it could not be possible to be friends with someone to whom you were previously attracted. Kate met Dick's ex-girlfriend, the longest and most meaningful relationship that he had prior to meeting Kate. Even though there was no reason for her to feel insecure, it still made her feel extremely uncomfortable.

A few months into their relationship, there was a lady that Dick had brought up in conversation often. Her name was Zara. Although Zara was dating a guy at the time, she was very close to Dick. Kate was invited to attend the first of many of Dick's work functions, and Dick had to excuse himself from the table to take a call from Zara who was in desperate need of relationship advice. Kate was quite annoyed that the call had to be taken even though Dick was at a function. Kate was also then left for a considerable amount of time with Dick's work colleagues as he spent at least an hour counselling Zara. Kate was shy, especially around new people that she had not met before, and Kate was the new buzz word in Dick's circle of friends. This made her feel as though she was under the spotlight.

Kate's family were having their traditional family New Year's Eve party, and so Kate's mum extended the invite to Dick and his family. Dick's brother was going to his girlfriend's house, and so Dick's mom and sister joined Dick and Kate for the evening. At the stroke of midnight, as everyone wished each other well for the New Year, Kate could not find Dick. Eventually, Kate stumbled upon Dick in her bedroom consoling his sister, who was crying uncontrollably. Dick asked Kate to give them a few minutes, and he would be out. Dick never shared with Kate what was being discussed and why his sister was crying, but Kate came to the educated deduction that she was upset that he had not been giving her the same time and attention as before Dick meeting Kate. Not long after that, Dick's sister left the party and went out to a nightclub with her friends.

Kate always chose to avoid situations in which she would have to voice her opinion, as this would lead to an argument with Dick. Kate was quite afraid of Dick. In very tough arguments, Kate would end up crying and this would very often be accompanied by an anxiety attack in which she would gasp for breath. Kate struggled to share her true thoughts, emotions and feelings with Dick. Dick would get frustrated and angry with Kate when she experienced an anxiety attack, and he would complain that they could never have a discussion because of her reaction. Kate, on the other hand, felt that she was never heard and that her opinion did not matter. Dick had an extremely strong character. He was very confident and not shy to share his point of view or opinion, but when it came down to the emotional or softer side of things, he was unresponsive in working through disagreements or openly sharing with Kate.

In the coming year, Dick would spend Sunday lunches with his family and visited Kate in the late afternoon, early evening. Later in the relationship, Kate was invited to join the lunches. Initially, time spent with Dick's family was nice. Kate seemed comfortable and would assist in the kitchen making salad, laying the table and doing the dishes. Kate was extremely shy and would often remember Dick's family commenting on what she was wearing and enquiring about which store she had purchased it from. This conversation would always make Kate feel awkward and uncomfortable, as she preferred maintaining her own unique style and did not understand why Dick's family needed to know such details. Kate had certainly not established a bond or relationship with Dick's mother or sister to be able to share openly with them yet. Kate had a sense that she was being judged and copied by Dick's sister and, to some extent, even his mother! Kate was in competition with no one, if only they could see this! Besides, there was an underlying perception that Kate was spoilt and had everything she desired as she came from a perceived-to-be wealthy family. One of the things that stood out was the fact that Dick's mother made it known that Kate had her own platinum credit card linked to her dad's account whilst in university. The focus on money and status of wealth made Kate feel uneasy, as she knew the only reason that she had this credit card was because her dad trusted her. It was solely for the purpose of purchasing textbooks on campus, and if any emergencies should arise. Kate's dad always ensured that their family was taken care of and, most importantly, Kate and her sister's education took priority. Kate and her sister attended schools that would provide them with a solid education and foundation should they wish to further their studies. They were privileged girls in that they did not have to seek any additional funding or bursary to further their studies.

Dick's background was different from Kate's in that he had paid his own way and put himself through tertiary education. After finishing high school, Dick had taken a gap year. The following year he attended a college in which he did basic computer training (A+, N+ etc.). His interest in computers stemmed from spending time with his dad whilst growing up. Ernst and Young visited the college that Dick attended and chose two individuals, one of which was Dick, and the other his friend, to go on and work for the company. This was the first door that opened for what was an amazing career that lay ahead for Dick. Dick started at a junior level, and, within eight years, worked his way up to a senior level. He studied his Bachelor of Commerce Informatics degree part-time through UNISA. Kate was extremely proud of Dick because he was the only one of three siblings that paid his own way to complete his degree and set himself up. He was extremely intelligent, outgoing, and did not have to work ridiculously hard to get ahead and succeed in the corporate world.

Kate and Dick spent a lot of time studying together initially as Kate completed her final year of university, and Dick continued with his bachelor's degree part-time. One afternoon, whilst studying, Dick started sketching a pattern of a wedding ring. The thought of planning what her wedding ring would look like excited Kate, as it would any girl. However, Dick led the design and influenced the final appearance of the ring, which portrayed a wave pattern that would be present on both of their rings. Kate's ring was simple and dainty, and she did not make a big fuss of what she wanted or the particular size of diamonds to be used. The design was completed and taken to Kate's family jeweller to create.

Kate's sister was expecting her first child in August 2004. Kate and Dick had agreed to do the traditional Hindu proposal which involved Dick's family coming over to ask her dad for her hand in marriage. Kate's only experience of such a proposal was her sister's proposal, which went off well, and Dick's brother's proposal that took place a few months prior to theirs. It was Friday the 13th August, and Kate was slightly nervous but still not very aware of what was to come or to be expected. Kate was under the impression that it would just be her parents, Dick's mother, Dick and her that actually had the discussion. Once the family arrived, the discussion got under way in front of siblings and partners. Dick's mother started highly confident and began by declaring the reason that Dick and his family were present was to ask for Kate's hand in marriage. Kate's dad responded by expanding into the upbringing of his daughters and providing for them to ensure that they were set up for life. Dick's mother did not receive the conversation very well and took offence that Kate's dad was implying that since she was a divorced, single woman, Dick and his siblings were not raised in a similar manner. The tension rose in the room, and Kate was extremely uncomfortable. Kate wished that her dad would have not talked so proudly of their upbringing and family values. Dick's brother's girlfriend held Kate's hand as the conversation continued. Kate was in a twilight zone and quite unsure of how to influence the discussion that was underway with various perceptions and interpretations at play. Once the formality was completed, the two families had dinner and the evening was concluded. Dick stayed longer and did not leave with his family. The moment that Dick and Kate found alone time, they discussed the evening, and both agreed that the evening did not go as they had planned. For one, Kate felt it would have been different if the discussion was just with their parents. That evening, Dick did not speak or share much about his thoughts on the content of the discussion. They were both comfortable in letting the event go as done.

However, the following day was a completely different story. Dick arrived home to an angry and upset mother. As his family drove out that evening, she began crying in the car. She shared with Dick's siblings and partners that she was furious that Kate's dad spoke to her the way that he did. She felt an attack on her parenting style and a judgement on the fact that she was a single mother raising her kids on her own. In no way did Kate's dad criticize her parenting technique, but this was unfortunately her perception and interpretation. If Kate's dad had any doubts about Dick's background or upbringing, the young couple would surely not have gotten to the stage of a marriage proposal. Dick was greatly influenced and manipulated by an upset and hurt mother. As a result, Dick bought into his mother's feelings and thoughts, and his opinion drastically changed. Dick was now in agreement that Kate's dad was wrong in the manner in which he spoke to his mother and family, making them feel unwelcomed.

Kate could not believe the sudden turn in their story, and the fact that the most important step in their journey ahead was nothing as she had envisaged it to be! Although Dick shared with Kate his mother's reaction and that he was in agreement with her, the couple did not discuss how they would fix the matter and just continued as normal. Kate, in turn, could not keep the disturbing news to herself, and so she shared it with her mum.

Kate's niece was born on the 26th August 2004. Kate's sister had sold their house and had not moved into their new house as yet. As a result, she ended up moving back home. Dick's mother did not call Kate's family to congratulate them on the birth of their first grandchild. Traditionally, Hindus partake in a naming ceremony on the 9th or 11th day after the baby's birth. Kate's mum had decided not to invite Dick's family since his mother was upset and no longer talking to them. Prior to the disastrous marriage proposal, the relationship between the parents was good, and Kate's mum strongly felt that Dick's mother could have picked up the phone and discussed the matter and the way that she felt.

On the Saturday after Kate's niece was born, Kate's dad went out for his morning cycle and was thrown off his bicycle by a taxi driver, resulting in his ankle being broken in three different places. He was in the hospital for the weekend and was discharged on the morning of the christening. Kate's brother-in-law went to go and fetch her dad from the hospital. Not too long after, Dick arrived. Kate was in her bedroom blow-drying her hair. Dick started probing her and enquiring how he should respond to any extended family that could potentially ask him where his mother and family were and why they were not at the event. Kate and Dick started to argue whilst her room door was open. Her sister then came in, and she started to lay into Dick. Kate's sister was never fond of Dick from the onset and did not think he was a match for her. This now just gave her reason to say what she truly felt about him as she was highly enraged. Kate's sister was notorious for lashing out and saying unreasonable things based on her emotions and feelings at the time. Kate's aunt then heard the commotion, and she jumped in as well!

Kate was terribly embarrassed by the situation that was just spiralling out of control. She was a dignified person and never imagined that her family would react in this manner. Kate's mum and grandmother came in to try and calm the situation. Kate could not explain the actions of her sister or aunt, or understand the reason for their behaviour. Once the situation calmed down, Dick prepared to leave the house. He told Kate it was over, and their relationship was done. He was extremely upset that Kate did not stand up to her family or say anything.

Kate was in extreme shock at what had just transpired in front of her own eyes. She understood her sister's reaction, but her aunt's support for her sister surprised her as she got along well with Dick and was extremely supportive of their relationship. Kate did not make any attempt to stop Dick from leaving.

Kate's family continued to get dressed for the function, and the day continued as normal as the guests arrived. Kate was physically present, but her mind was clouded. The incident was not discussed further amongst her family. Kate spoke to Jane about it, and her aunt tried to console her.

In the week to follow, Kate's mum received a call from the family jeweller out of concern as he had received a call from Dick to cancel the order on the engagement ring! Kate's mum was surprised, but the news made sense to Kate given the misfortune that had unfolded on the morning of her niece's christening.

In the days to come, Jane would chat to Dick at work and play a supportive role. She tried to understand how come Dick was adamant that the relationship was over just because of the incident. Jane knew how deeply Dick felt about Kate, that he had never met a woman like Kate, and wanted to marry her and have her be the mother of his children one day. In conjunction, Jane would also chat to Kate and see if she was willing to work through the challenges that the couple were faced with. After a week of separation and no communication, Jane convinced both Kate and Dick to meet.

Dick was very firm in his position and still upset that Kate did not stand up for him in front of her family. He did not understand Kate's point of view, and that she too was in complete shock and did not know how to react as the heated situation unfolded. The preceding factors that contributed to the blow-out were one-sided. Dick was not willing to believe that Kate's dad's intention was never to make his mother feel uncomfortable or any less. Kate had never dealt with such a situation before; it was a tough one in which she needed to stand up to her family in support of her boyfriend or else go against them. Dick gave Kate an ultimatum. He would only be willing to work through things with her on the condition that he not have any connection or relationship with Kate's sister or aunt. Kate was embarrassed by their conduct and felt this was understandable, and so she agreed. Dick was still upset about the proposal, which in retrospect seemed to be the underlying root cause. However, Kate's family's appalling behaviour now took precedence, and the proposal was in the distant past.

Kate prepared herself. She decided to have a mature discussion with her parents and, more importantly, explain to her dad what had happened on the morning of her niece's christening from her perspective. Kate explained how Dick's mother had interpreted the proposal, and how this then led to Dick's family not being invited to the christening. Kate expressed that it was an extremely tricky situation, and she wished to work things out with Dick. Kate's sister overheard the conversation with her parents, stormed into the room and gave Kate the ultimatum that if she was to pursue a relationship with Dick, she would disown her. Kate reassured her that the choice to be a part of her life was entirely hers; however, it was Kate's life at the end of the day, and she had decided to work things out with Dick.

Kate had a close mentor in her accounting high school teacher, who in later years became a big part of her personal life. She advised Kate to go and see Dick's mum and apologise to her for the way that Kate's dad made her feel. Without Dick's knowledge, Kate took her teacher's advice and, one afternoon after university, drove to Dick's mother's home and apologised. Kate was extremely proud of herself as it took a lot of courage to reach out to Dick's mother without having any indication of how this might end. Dick's mother accepted the apology. Kate was so relieved and excited to share her courageousness with Dick!

Kate and Dick agreed that he too should meet with her parents to clear the air. The meeting with Kate's parents went well, and at least it seemed as though both sets of parents were now okay with the young couple pursuing their relationship. The parents, however, still did not make any contact with each other.

The last stretch of Kate's degree turned out to be trying given the tension at home post the awkward proposal. Kate graduated at the end of 2004 with incredibly good grades. Kate's sister was barely talking to her at the time, as she was still upset that Kate was pursuing her relationship with Dick. Kate attended her graduation with her parents and Dick. Dick had bought her a bunch of flowers and gave her a photo frame. The frame held the first photo of Dick that Jane shared prior to the couple's first date.

Kate and Dick had decided that they would get engaged in January 2005 and court-registered by March of 2005. It was the day before Dick's birthday, and Kate had a feeling that this was the day he was going to propose. Kate's parents were away for a weekend break, and Dick had planned to take her for a drive out into the countryside near the Hartebeespoort Dam. Kate, however, was not excited in anticipation for the proposal and just went along with the flow. Dick drove to the aerial cable way in Hartebeespoort, and this is where Dick indeed popped the question! As they made their way up to the top and found a quiet spot, Dick went down on one knee and took out a piece of paper from his pocket. Dick held Kate's hand as he read what he had written. Dick had the ability to write very well and convey his feelings eloquently. Kate listened to Dick's declaration of love filled with the perfect wording; however, she felt ordinary. There were no butterflies in her stomach, and

Dick was not sweeping her off her feet. As time stood still, Kate did not identify with the moment and sadly this was not how she would have envisaged someone declaring their love for her and asking her to marry him. Her expectations were set high after the romantic setting in which she received her promise ring. But when the time came for her to respond to the question … she said yes! After saying yes, Kate felt all sorts of emotions. There was uncertainty and a little bit of anxiety. How was she to share this information with her parents and family? At the same time, something within her allowed her to say yes. Somehow a bigger force was at play.

Dick strangely did not have a lunch date planned, and the couple were chilled for the day. It felt like an ordinary Sunday besides having a beautiful fourteen-carat white gold engagement ring on her finger.

Kate called her parents to share the news, and it was extremely quiet on the receiver. The couple decided to go to Kate's cousin's house to share the news, but again it was almost like an anti-climax to what was supposedly meant to be good news. The trying relationship continued; Dick and Kate were now engaged and to be registered in a couple of months' time.

The traditional Hindu wedding ceremony was planned for the following April. However, Dick and Kate planned to have their court registration undertaken the previous March in the hope that Kate would not have to travel far out of Johannesburg to perform her community service post her internship. Kate and Dick got registered at the Melrose temple on the 15th March 2005. The priest at the temple was a marriage commissioner, and the anti-nuptial wedding contract followed later. The witnesses at the temple were Jane and a friend of Kate's. After the signing was done at the temple, the couple went home to a lovely dinner prepared by Kate's mum. Kate wore a lilac traditional saree and her grandmother's necklace: it was the most special piece that day.

It was done, Kate was legally married to Dick!

Kate saved every cent from her second pay check onwards toward their wedding. Whilst Kate's dad was going to pay for a good portion of the wedding, Kate did not want to take advantage of this offering and decided to save towards the wedding to make a significant contribution. As a result, this also afforded Dick and Kate the opportunity to have a special honeymoon which Dick funded as he did not have to contribute toward the wedding.

Much of 2005, Kate spent planning her dream wedding. Kate and Dick went alone on weekends viewing venues and deciding which would suit them. The couple chose a venue with magnificent gardens and a quaint little river running through it. The surroundings were truly tranquil, peaceful and filled with local birds and ducks. The setting was beautiful! The date was set, the 16th April 2006, at Makiti in Muldersdrift.

Kate and Dick discussed the opportunity to work abroad for a brief period. The couple attended a seminar on job offers for Dick's industry, and they came across the island of Bermuda. After much research, this destination proved to be the most suited to Kate's career versus other countries which had prerequisites for pharmacists. Therefore, the couple set out to look for a two-year work contract starting in 2007.

CHAPTER 3
A Fairy-Tale Wedding

Every girl dreams of a fairy-tale wedding, and Kate was no different in this regard. It all begins with reading childhood stories that influence the picture of what a girl imagines her prince in shining armour to look like and what her fairy-tale wedding day would be. Kate always dreamt of getting married in a white dress, which is not traditional for those following the Hindu faith. Dick's dad was from Northern India, and his family followed slightly different traditions to Kate's family background which originated from the south of India. The wedding ceremony was to take place following the Hindi tradition. Kate's mum would have loved for her to follow their tradition of course, but this was not the case. Indians traditionally have many rituals leading up to the actual wedding ceremony. Since this had to be performed slightly differently or in ways Kate's family were not familiar with, her mum was under tremendous pressure with the mammoth preparations that were required. Not to forget, she also had a daughter that was being pedantic about every little detail!

A Hindu wedding is a wonderful celebration of bright colours, family, food, tradition and dance. Traditional Hindu weddings have guest lists that extend into over thousands of people being invited by both families. The traditional wedding ceremony is never in English, and most people that attend Indian weddings do not pay attention to the couple taking their vows. Given these factors, Kate and Dick rather invited only immediate family, namely their siblings, grandparents and those that were required to partake in the actual ceremony. All other guests were only invited to the wedding reception.

There was not a single detail that Kate did not spend time and effort on. She had scrapbooked the outside of the printed wedding invitations and had hand-created the table settings. Kate had chosen a clay, earthy colour for her wedding saree. It was simple, with dainty beadwork and embellishments, but rather elegant. Dick's kurta outfit matched perfectly, adorned with a scarf that complimented Kate's wedding veil.

The wedding rituals started two days before the actual wedding. The first day was the Mehndi evening. Mehndi holds a lot of cultural significance within Indian traditions. Mehndi or henna is a paste created from the powdered leaf of the henna plant. Kate's hands and feet were decorated with an intricate pattern that she had chosen. Kate was spoilt that evening, as she was hand-fed by her cousins as she could not use her hands. She was even more spoilt by her mum who had to assist her on the loo! Kate had to sleep with the paste on overnight, and it was only to be washed off the next morning.

The Mehndi ceremony signifies beautification of the bride-to-be. The female relatives of the family also apply mehndi on their palms to take part in the celebrations. The colour of mehndi is given high importance within the Indian culture as the darkness of the colour signifies the degree of the husband and mother-in-law's love. It depicts the love and affection between the couple and, as it is believed, the longer it is retained on the skin, the more auspicious it is. Surprisingly, Kate's mehndi was removed on the first few days of their honeymoon and did not last as long as she expected. Kate of course assigned this to the seawater and the theory that perhaps the saltiness had removed it!

The day before the wedding, two particularly important Indian rituals take place, namely the *thiluk* and *hurdee* ceremony also known as the cleansing or purification ceremony.

Thiluk ceremony:

The thiluk ceremony takes place at the groom's house. The bride's family arrives in a procession bearing fruits, gifts and other Indian traditional sweetmeats and delights. The bride's brother must wash the groom's feet and put a dot (thiluk) on the groom's forehead as a symbol of accepting and welcoming him into the family on behalf of his sister. This part of the ceremony was done by Kate's close cousin as she did not have a brother.

Hurdee ceremony:

A paste of hurdee, which is created from turmeric bark that is ground to form a paste, is applied on the bride and groom's faces and entire body the day before the wedding day. This ceremony is held in parallel at both the bride's and groom's homes. The hurdee is meant to act as a purifier and makes the bride and groom's skin glow and illuminate on the day of the wedding. Usually, only women participate in this ceremony but in modern times this day is filled with fun, enjoyment and laughter amongst close friends and relatives, both males and females joining in on the ceremony.

The bride also performs a tradition whereby a hole is dug in the ground and camphor blocks are lit, whilst the hole is enclosed with flowers. This tradition is in praise of Mother Earth and asking for her blessing to ensure that all goes well on the wedding day.

The end of the hurdee ceremony is concluded with a meal and lots of dance and celebration with family and friends.

After two days filled with many rituals, not much sleep and the anxiety of making sure it all went off smoothly, Kate was feeling tired. The wedding ceremony started at 10:00 in Muldersdrift. Kate had to be up incredibly early to shower, wash off all the hurdee and be ready for the lady that was coming to do her hair, make-up and drape her saree. It was a lot that had to be prepped, which meant Kate needed to be wide awake at 4:00. This would allow enough time for photographs and travel time to the venue too!

Kate could not believe that the day had arrived, and she was going to be married in just a few hours. Kate did not plan on saying a speech at the wedding reception and, therefore, had written a letter to her parents to tell them how much she loved them and how grateful she was for all that they had provided her with and their assistance in moulding her into the lady she had become.

"16/04/2006

Dearest Mum and Dad,

This is something just for the two of you from me! I preferred to do this as I feel it is more intimate and special as compared to saying this in front of one hundred and ninety-three guests. It is also my request that no one else but the two of you read this.

The two of you are the most amazing people that I could ever have been blessed with. I have been so fortunate in everything that you have provided me with, the list is endless!

Dad my thank yous will never be enough, and I will forever be indebted to you! Thank you for supporting and guiding me throughout my education, primary, secondary, and tertiary. Thank you for being so hard on me to always push to do my best and succeed! Today I can sit back and say I have truly achieved both what you and I would have liked me to have. Thank you for teaching me the meaning of hard work, dedication, commitment, punctuality, good morals and principles by which I can live my life by today! I know I have not said it as often as I may have wanted to but Dad you would never really know how much I truly love you and how grateful I am for all that you've done for me and continue to do for me!

Mum, thank you for being my confidant, my best friend, my sister, the shoulder that I could always cry on, the ears that always listened to me, the one that always gave me the confidence to do the things that I never thought possible. Thank you for all the lovely lunch boxes that you always packed for me that everyone always envies. Thank you for those nights when you sat up with me till the early hours in the study.

Thanks for all the hard work that has gone into preparing for this wedding. I know it has been stressful for us, but it will be an amazing function that we can be proud of!

This is a such a huge step that I take now as I try to emulate what Dad and You have taught me as I start out with Dick to form our own family. I am so sad to leave the two of you, your'll do not know how much I'm going to miss your'll but at least I know that your'll still have each other.

I have mixed feelings at this moment of excitement, sadness, anxiety, fear ...

I know your'll are also probably sad with me leaving at the end of the year but it's something that I have to do and at least your'll will have a holiday destination to go to now that Dad is retired and before we know it the four years will be over.

I pray that God will look after the two of you and always bless and protect your'll.

I love you both so much more than words can ever express.

Kate "

The lady that did Kate's hair, make-up and saree draping was so talented and amazing. She was in a car accident a few years beforehand. Her hand was injured, but she did a spectacular job of making Kate look absolutely beautiful! Kate's make-up was done perfectly, with an absolute natural look that allowed her inner beauty to shine through.

The morning of the wedding was slightly cloudy, which was unexpected for that time of the year in Johannesburg, but as the lovely bride drove through the entrance gate, the clouds started to move.

Kate had to sit in the chapel as she awaited the arrival of the groom and his family. The first ritual to take place was with the women of both families joining in for a light-hearted game which was played to signify the welcoming of the families.

Kate then walked down the red-carpet to the draped wrought-iron gazebo that stood just in front of the meander of water, hand-in-hand with her dad who couldn't have been prouder of his little girl. Dick stood in front of the altar with the largest and most fulfilled smile on his face.

The ceremony then began. A Hindu priest led Kate and Dick, and their families through the sacrament of marriage. In the Hindu religion, all new beginnings are marked by the auspicious havan. The havan, also known as agni, is the sacred fire created from woollen wicks, wooden sticks and ghee (butter). It is symbolic of light, energy and purity, and is regarded as the chief witness to the wedding. Mantras are chanted inviting the various deities to be present, witness and bless the wedding.

Exchanging of garlands made from fresh flowers is a significant part of the wedding ceremony. An Indian marriage is not considered to be complete until the bride and groom exchange their garlands. This is symbolic of unifying two souls into one.

Among the various sacred rites exists the ritual of the seven pheras (encirclements), considered one of the most sacred and significant ritual of the Hindu wedding ceremony. Seven pheras, also called Saptapadi (in the Sanskrit language), refer to the ceremony of the bridal couple walking seven times around the sacred fire. The priest utters aloud religious mantras as the bridal couple walks around the fire.

The significance of each of the pheras:

The first phera:

In the first phera, the couple pray to the Creator to extend his blessings on the bridal couple in the form of striving for a respectful life and always having the provision of healthy food. The first phera also indicates that the Creator is the only ultimate deity who can bless the couple with great benefit of an honourable life and wholesome food on the table always.

The groom's pledge by performing the first phera is that with each passing day their love for each other shall become more intense. They will help each other in every possible way. The bride will cook for him, and he will bestow his love and affection upon her and always shower her with goodness during their journey of married life. He will treat her kindly and promise to keep her happy, healthy and loved always.

The bride's pledge is to wholeheartedly accept the groom's judgement. She promises to fulfil her responsibilities as the heart of the family and take care of their family with the utmost care and dedication. The bride will take care of the groom's honour and remain abided by his love forever.

The second phera:

In the second phera, the couple pleads to the Creator to impart them with mental stability, physical health and spiritual strength so that they can live their lives smoothly after their new relation as husband and wife.

The groom's pledge by performing this phera is to promise to each other that they will stand by each other forever. The bride will be the initiating strength and courage. Together, they will be able to defend their home and family against all odds and any evil.

The bride's pledge is to always fill the groom's heart with exuberant courage and strength. She will only ever utter pleasant words that shall be supporting of their family and children from any evil. The groom shall love her as his life partner.

The third phera:

In the third phera, the bridal couple asks the Creator to provide them with the utmost wisdom, wealth and prosperity so that they can encounter a contented and satisfied life forever after. The third phera also signifies the importance of religious and sacred responsibility which shall be performed by the couple in their future.

The groom's pledge in performing this phera to his bride is to promise that they will remain spiritually abided by each other. He will only look to other women as sisters. They will grow and flourish together under the sacred and holy sanctity of the Creator.

The bride's pledge is to love the groom for her entire life. She will only consider other men as brothers. Her love and respect for him shall never fade. By virtue of her love and devotion, she will remain his faithful wife.

The fourth phera:

In the fourth phera, the couple prays to the Creator for bestowing happiness and a bond between them. The fourth phera also signifies the importance of family, parents and elders. The fourth phera brings out a commitment between two souls that they will remain pledged to take care of their elders, family members and parents for the rest of their lives.

The groom's pledge is to promise each other that they will provide utmost aid to their elders and parents. The bride will bring good fortune and sanctity to the groom's life. May the Creator bless the couple with a blissful life and healthy children.

The bride's pledge is to decorate and adorn herself with jewellery, flowers and garlands just for the groom. The euphoria of her fragrance will be bestowed only upon the groom. She will serve and please him in every way possible.

The fifth phera:

In the fifth phera, the couple pray that the Creator will bless them with kindness for all living things of this universe. They pray for the happiness and well-being of each other's relatives and friends. The fifth phera denotes the bridal couple's concern with each other's family members and relatives. It also signifies the moral responsibilities toward the charities and universal welfare. They also pray for honourable offspring.

The groom's pledge is having walked the four steps together, the bride has already enriched his life. He asks that she be blessed with all happiness and may her loved ones live a long and happy life. He invites her to come and share his duties for all charity acts in order for them to enrich their family and be blessed with noble, righteous and brave children.

The bride's pledge is to always be with her groom in all circumstances. She will share his joy, happiness and grievances. His love will give her strength and the trust to respect him. Her utmost concern will be to fulfil all his wishes. She will do her utmost to carry out all of his wishes.

The sixth phera:

By performing the sixth phera, the couple implore for a long and happy life together. They pray to the Creator to extend his blessings for a long-lived togetherness. Their wish is to enjoy plentiful and endless seasons with each other. The sixth phera is completely related to the long, joyous life and oneness.

The groom declares that the bride has added immense happiness to his life by taking these six steps with him. His heart is filled with joy, and he always wishes to have her by his side. May she always be a part of his life filling it with pleasure and peace.

The bride replies and confirms that she will always walk beside her groom and that she will participate in all of his honourable acts. She will stand by him to perform the jobs and tasks that will enrich their prosperity and abundance. She will also extend her efforts to all of his devotional duties.

The seventh phera:

The seventh phera is the last phera. In the seventh phera, the bride and groom ask for a joyful life. The couple requests that the Creator marks them a long-lasting bond enriched with good understanding, loyalty and companionship. They pledge to bear the relationship with love and honesty. The couple prays for universal world peace and social welfare.

The groom states that they have performed all seven pheras together and now have a single identity. Hence after, they would be incomplete without each other. Their existence will be entirely devoted to each other. He declares that he is completely hers, and she is completely his. May their bond be perpetual and their marriage everlasting.

The bride declares that it is a privilege to be his wife, and she promises to always be truthful. She declares that they will always love each other. Given all the promises that they have taken in this holy ritual, they will do their utmost best to carry out the same with the purest intentions. They pledge to be transparent with each other in all that they do going forward.

After the completion of the seven pheras follows the Kanya Daan ritual.

Kanya Daan:

The kanya daan ritual means "giving away the bride," and is performed by the bride's parents. The father of the bride takes his daughter's right hand and places it in the groom's right hand, requesting him to accept his daughter as an equal partner. This ritual signifies both the acceptance of the bride's father and his official approval to give his daughter away. After joining the two hands, the mother of the bride pours sacred water onto the palm of her husband's hands allowing it to flow through his fingers onto his daughter's hand below and ultimately to the groom's hand below as well. It is said that the father of the bride has to give away his most precious possession – his daughter – in order for the bride to receive great prosperity and good fortune for her future.

After the observation of the kanya daan, the groom's sister ties the end of his scarf to the bride's saree with betel nuts, copper coins and rice symbolizing unity, prosperity and happiness for the couple. The knot represents the eternal bond that comes with marriage.

Sindoor is a traditional vermillion red or orange-red powder that is worn by married women in the centre parting of their hair. The groom places the sindoor on the bride's forehead and in the front parting of her hair. The groom is required to do this for the first time during the wedding ceremony.

The priest had requested that Kate needed to wear this sindoor powder for the first forty days of marriage. Kate decided to get Dick to place the sindoor on her forehead for the first forty days, and she then continued to wear this sacred powder for every day of her marriage. Most people found this surprising, as it is not common in western society these days to see Hindu women follow this tradition. Kate was of the belief that if you are going to do something, always ensure it is done properly or not done at all!

It is suggested that the red colour symbolises power. According to Hindu tradition, a woman has to adorn sindoor until her husband passes on. It is believed that the ritual protects the husbands of all married women who wear sindoor and wards off any evil spirits.

Mangalsutra:

In Sanskrit, mangal means "holy, auspicious" and sutra means "thread". A mangalsutrais is a necklace that a Hindu groom secures around the bride's neck in a ceremony called mangalya dharanam which identifies her as a married woman.

And that was the traditional Hindu wedding ceremony concluded. The first to bless the bridal couple were the grandparents, and then the parents of each side. The couple bows down and asks for the elders' blessings. The invited guests then congratulate the couple and shower them with fresh flower petals.

After the wedding ceremony, the last Hindu tradition is the bride bidding farewell to her family as she leaves to go to her husband's house for the first time as his new bride. Once the couple reach the groom's house, as the bride enters through the doorway, the bride knocks over a metal pot filled with uncooked rice using her right foot. Together the couple go to the prayer room and say a prayer.

Kate and Dick then made their way back to the wedding venue for an afternoon photoshoot in the beautiful gardens. An hour was set aside prior to the guests arriving for the wedding reception. Kate and Dick were comfortable with each other in front of the cameras and, as a result, they completed the photoshoot in just under forty-five minutes. It was the photographer's first occasion shooting an Indian wedding and, as such, he had loads of fun capturing all the various moments and traditions for Kate and Dick.

The bridal couple then welcomed all their guests to the reception for the occasion that everyone had been waiting for. Kate and Dick stayed in their bridal outfits for those that had not been present at the morning wedding ceremony. After the initial welcome, Kate and Dick went off to change into their outfits for the reception.

The reception room boasted high ceilings which culminated into thatch roofing. The beams in the ceiling were beautifully draped with white fabric which all cascaded down and met in the midpoint, crowned with an elaborate chandelier. The table settings were simple but elegant, consisting of a shallow, glass dish filled with water reinforced by a wrought iron stand. In it were Gerber flowers in orange, yellow, crimson, peach and clay hues, and floating candles.

Kate and Dick did not have a main or family table set up due to the family disagreement prior to the wedding, and so Kate and Dick had their very own main table; just the two of them sat in the front of the room. Whilst Kate and Dick were the centre of attention for the day, they did seem to be microscopic in a considerable open space, perhaps a representation of this next step out into the great big world.

The master of ceremonies for the evening was Jane. Dick convinced Kate that they should not do many speeches. Kate was sure that Dick was shying away from having family speak on their behalf, and most certainly him not wanting her dad to say anything. Besides a vote of thanks done on Kate's behalf by her cousin, Dick's speech was the only speech for the evening. His speech was forty-five minutes long! It was by far the longest groom's speech Kate had listened to, but it was extremely descriptive and entertaining, to say the least. The guests were in laughter for most of it!

Good evening everyone. So now for the good news, bad news, the worse news and the worst news.

The good news - there is only one speech for the evening.

The bad news - I have a microphone in my hand.

The worse news - I'm about to give a speech.

The worst news - It's going to be a long one.

So please make sure that all tray tables are secured, all seats are in the upright position, all seat belts are fastened, and all luggage is stored securely underneath your seat.

The best place to start with a speech like this is gratitude. I would like to thank four parties in particular:

The first of which are our honoured guests, both family and friends. When Kate and I made our guest list, we thought of people who take a personal interest in our lives and are genuinely a part of it. If you are sitting in this hall then you are definitely important to us, and we thank you for making the difference in our lives that allowed us to have you as our guests. I mean, if it wasn't for all of you, a function like this, and I think everyone knows what I'm getting at, a function like this would have cost a whole lot less…Just joking, I kid, I kid. No really, we thank all of you, those who have travelled from far and wide, and I'm not even talking about the out-of-towners because this place is really far away. Thanks for the gifts we have received and, no matter how big or small, above all else Kate and I truly cherish your presence here with us.

The second group that deserve thanks are our families. For me personally, I really can't put into words what my family means to me. To my mom who has been the inspiration and grounding of my very soul. A mother's love is like no other; you embody and define that very expression in a way that I wish I could attempt in the fatherly love that I will one day show my children. You are a primary reason for the man I have become and that has led to this day. You have beaten all odds to be where you are today and to bring up the children you have. To my brother, Simon you are a true gentleman well ahead of your years. You are exactly what an older brother/sibling has to embody; there is still so much that I can learn from you. Michelle, what can I say about the best friend of my life? Your maturity is so well beyond your years, it scares me. I wish you all the best in your life and know that you will achieve greatness. You are a gem and don't forget all that is our bond. Growing up, I never needed anything besides the immediate company of my family, my best friends. Home was my centre, and you all were my home. This step I take into this new life is only a natural progression from the love-filled life we've led, and I can never thank you all enough for what I have been given. We have come a long hard way, but it's all been more than worth it. A home is not made of bricks and mortar, it is made of love!

To our families, if it wasn't for the way both Kate and I were brought up, we would never have fallen in love with each other. So, this marriage is a product of our upbringing. Thank you so much. Thanks for the acceptance that we have been afforded in both families that makes the fact that we are now officially daughter and son-in-law nothing but a mere formality.

The third group, or should I say person, to thank is very special. The reason everyone sits here today is because of her. She is a truly amazing person who has blessed Kate and I. Who am I talking about but the delightful Ms. Jane of course! The MC. And by MC I mean, the 'main charou'. Let me tell you about this lady, and you will understand why her passion is in human beings. Jane and I worked in the same company for a long time but had never formally spoken. She eventually joined our division. Within the first month of her being there, we had gone on a training course facilitated by her. Jane and I instantly got along. I had barely known Jane as we spent minimal time together. She thought 'hey', this guy would make a great match for this girl I know. Kate was that girl. Just as remarkable though, Jane didn't know Kate in depth either. She just knew that they would make a match. One thing led to another and if it wasn't for her foresight, they would not be here today. Jane, you have afforded Kate and I the chance of many lifetimes. You have made a match even heaven would blink at. Thank you so much for the support you have lent both of us, and we hope that the happiness you have presented us returns to you over and over and over. You will always have the most special place in our hearts and lives because you were responsible for US.

Before I give this thanks, I'd like to tell you the story of us:

So, Jane and I sit and talk every day at work, and one day she shows me this picture of this hotty. I'm like hey, I'm single and I really don't mind meeting someone. She looks pretty good, so how's about a hook up. Ok, so it wasn't exactly in that tone, but I just want you to understand the cool guy I was! Sure! Anyway, it was decided that there would be an exchange of pictures between Kate and I and we'd take it from there. So, I sent Jane a couple of pics, and she chooses the best ones. Obviously, I disagreed but hey, I needed female intuition here. These development stages are so important not to mess up. After Kate got the picture, she sounded interested and we started emailing. More like me begging to meet her. As you well know, Kate is quite the diligent student. Between her studies, Idols 'at the time' and the fact that I wasn't Jonty Rhodes, it would take some serious grovelling to get to see her. And when it comes to grovelling, there's no competition. I had convinced Kate how much it's in her best interest to see me and after about a week, it was done. I must admit, I did have some help. It's called devilish good looks!!! Apparently, the picture of me was so hot that every time Kate looked at it, she had to have a cold shower. Anyway, she thought I was really hot because of my picture; she even printed it on her colour printer so that it was easily accessible. Now the reason I am building myself up here is because there's a huge fall coming. And that's why my nose is so big, permanent long-term damage kind of fall. So, eventually I convinced Kate to meet, obviously at the most romantic place in South Africa, Sandton City. I patiently waited inside the CNA sweating profusely, thinking what this first meeting would be like. I eventually decide to see if she's waiting by the beautiful rendezvous spot, also known as the glass rails in front of 'Sweets from Heaven'. Now guys, if you're going to meet a girl, a bit of advice. Although this happened by accident, try to approach her without her seeing you so that you can get a great big scope of that sexy ass. And boy did I enjoy that 10 seconds. I guess I wouldn't have enjoyed it for two reasons, if the girl that turned around was not Kate or if Kate didn't have a license to carry the sexy behind she had. But

*yes, to my absolute joy, it was her! When she turned around
and I saw what she really looks like, this is the face I made.
I hope she hadn't seen it cos I'd look pretty damn stupid.
Man was she so much hotter than her picture! Now, at this
point, I was already rating myself as 'the man', praying that
she would have the best personality and would, by an act
of God, fall head over heels in love with me. Anyway, so we
go to this romantic restaurant, Baglios and sit down to have
some ice cream and coffee. Unfortunately, it was coffee only
as no one wants to be on a first date with food or dessert in
their mouth. Within a few seconds of sitting down, there it
was, the one characteristic that blew me completely away.
Kate has the most amazing smile I have ever seen. It is so
wide that to look at it completely, you have to be a distance
far enough away so that your peripheral vision could cap-
ture it all. So, all I did was concentrate on that smile, making
sure it never subsided. She laughed a lot, and I prayed a lot.
All in all, just hoping that she thought I was great. So as the
conversation continues, she tells me how much she loves
South African Idols and thinks that Waafiq and Nazneen
are amazing and that she can't wait to get home in time for
Idols. It was like three hours away, and she only stayed 15
minutes away. Something was not right. So, we finished our
drink, and I walked her to the car looking like a smitten little
boy. So, after this Kate gets home and texts me after Idols.
Now, I am waiting for her to tell me what an out of this world
guy I am and here comes the start of the fall!!! So, she says,
'please vote for Nazneen and Waafiq.' That was it. I was
screwed. I've been looking like a lovesick puppy; my family
can't believe after just one small meeting that I can look like
this. Only to find out from Jane the next day that Kate thinks
I'm cute and have a great personality. Hmmm guys, have we
not heard of that one before. And later, I found out that the
cute part was conveniently added in by Jane. So, all I was,
was a walking great personality. So, after many texts of Kate
trying to figure out if I was really the guy in the picture and
me trying to get another meeting, we finally met a second*

time. She laughed so much that she thought, hey, I could be with this guy; he might not be that good looking, all I'd have to do is keep the picture close by for inspiration. Soon enough, I asked her out. But best of all, I found the defining factor that she was looking for, it's called no bog-bath (for a physical effect to look older of course!). The day that I shaved, Kate was her very own plaything. She would just stare at me and say I found the boy in the photo. Man did I lap it up! One month of going out, both head over heels in love and a promise ring later, everything was cast in stone just like that.

I've never known love until I met Kate. She has given me the gift of love. How do I explain to all of you what I feel for her or what she does for me? It is called poetry. Now in my lifetime, I have read a total of four books, two by choice. So, my vocabulary is completely based on thousands of movies I've watched in my lifetime. When I met Kate, it was a verse I wrote about her smile that knocked her completely off her feet and made her see through the thickness of my facial hair. And from that day onwards, it flowed through me like the love I feel for her. Everyone in this room knows of something that I wrote, and everyone has read it. And with this verse, I would like to propose a toast to the most amazing woman I have ever met! My best friend, my better half, my companion, my soulmate and, most importantly now, my wife! I look forward to a life filled with absolute love and contentment with you. So, with this verse I am still in awe of your absolute beauty; you more than complete me as I am overflowing beyond the brim. With this verse, I toast to you:

'What is love?
When the word was created
It knew nothing of You and I
It knows nothing of what we feel
Love is but only a glimpse
Of what I feel for You

And what you feel for Me
What we have is more than
Love could ever show
For now, and always
I more than love you
My Angel'

Kate and Dick's wedding cake comprised of two suitcases stacked one on top of the other, and an Indian bridal couple sat at the top of the uppermost suitcase. It was unique in that it was an Indian bridal couple, and the colours and style of their outfits accurately depicted Kate and Dick's actual outfits. The bridal couple cut the cake, and Dick fed her a piece of cake, and all was going as smoothly as could go.

Dick had decided that their wedding song would be "Everything" by Lifehouse. He confirmed with the DJ twice to make sure that he had the song, and the DJ confirmed that he did. About an hour before their first dance as a married couple, the DJ went to tell Dick that he did not have the song! Kate liked the lyrics of the song as it had a lot of meaning, but it definitely was not her first choice! The song that Kate and Dick chose to walk into the reception room with was Andrea Bocelli and Céline Dion, "The Prayer". To Dick's disappointment, they had no choice but to go with this song again as the song that they would do their first dance to.

Kate's dad sorted out the bill for the wedding. They had a cash bar facility, and immediate families were going to run their own tab as they were sitting at separate tables. Dick had a huge argument with Kate when she mentioned this to him again because it came up that Dick's brother did not have his credit card on him, and Dick was expecting Kate's dad to pay for their family bill as well! Kate was not concerned over the cost of the bill, but rather that the agreement was made between her and Dick, and that it was now being changed once Dick's family got involved. Kate could not believe that this was happening already on their wedding day. Dick was very firm with her, and he was becoming aggravated. Kate started to cry, and it was difficult to control it. This all unfolded right before the couple's first dance. The photographer captured the moment perfectly as Kate looked into the camera lens and smiled, whilst tears streamed down her face. Not everyone that would have seen this photo in their wedding album would ever have known the true meaning of the tears...it was not tears of joy or love but rather pain and fear.

This song gave Kate goose bumps and, ironically, it ended up being a truly relevant and appropriate song for the life that Kate and Dick led together.

The DJ did a great job for the rest of the evening, and everyone had a fantastic time. Kate had several friends and family members that wanted to buy her many shots. It is tradition for the bridal couple to be vegetarian for the day and abstain from alcohol. Half an hour until the last dance, Kate went and asked her mum whether it would be okay for her to drink the shots since the day was almost over. Since Dick did not drink any alcohol, Kate had to take double shots for both of them! Given that Kate had not drank any alcohol for the previous three years because of Dick's wishes, it did not take much to get her drunk! At the end of the last dance ... Dick's worst nightmare turned into a reality; his new bride was officially drunk!

Dick had to carry Kate over the wedding threshold and into their honeymoon suite for the night. Kate was uncertain whether this was out of choice or purely because she could not stand or walk on her own two feet! Dick was looking forward to their wedding night with great anticipation as their marriage would be consummated. This, unfortunately, was not the case. Instead, Dick found himself taking care of Kate. He had to undo her hair and take out the thousands of hairclips that were holding it up. They also spent most of the time doing this on the bathroom floor next to the toilet pan. Kate could not keep anything down and, once everything was out, she kept on retching. She felt extremely ill and awful, and eventually passed out cold. Dick was petrified, and was worried that he could not hear her breathing. Kate's body temperature had dropped a lot, and he spent the rest of the evening making sure she was alive and breathing! This was the first and last time Dick took care of Kate after a big night out, not that it happened very often!

The next morning, the deed was done. It was not exactly how Kate anticipated it to be! But then again, everyone does say that the first time is not like anything you expect it to be?! More excitingly though, Kate focused her thoughts to their honeymoon that was due to begin in a few hours' time as they made their way to the airport!

CHAPTER 4
Heaven on Earth

Dick took on the task of planning their honeymoon and informed Kate that they were going on a skiing trip to the Swiss Alps. As such, Kate had packed her suitcase complete with winter apparel. As they checked in for their flight, the lady asked if the bags were to be checked directly to Malé. Kate immediately said to Dick the destination did not sound like somewhere in the Alps; however, he insisted that the lady mispronounced the end destination and with a posh accent corrected her.

Kate and Dick had drinks with the family prior to boarding, which ended with Kate's two-year-old niece accidently spilling an entire glass of mango juice on Kate's corduroy pants! Once Kate and Dick were done saying goodbye to their family, they rushed through the security check as she needed to go and buy herself a new pair of pants. After going through passport control, Kate realised that she had forgotten to take their jackets from her mum, who was holding onto them! Dick reassured her it was fine and that they would buy new jackets when they got there! Kate was not complaining at all, any reason to shop for new clothing!

And so, they got to their first destination which was Dubai International Airport in transit to Malé. It was in Dubai that Dick confirmed that they were actually off to the Maldives! Kate was ecstatic and horrified at the same time … her suitcase was completely filled with winter apparel! Dick reassured her that her mum had repacked her suitcase, and it was all sorted! Kate was set! What more could a girl dream off? Newly married and off to the Maldives.

Kate and Dick arrived in Malé, which was a typical island with the usual tropical climate, and extremely hot and humid weather. They took an hour-long speedboat to their athol. The Maldives is made up of many athols, which are essentially small islands. Kate and Dick arrived at their resort, called Meeru, and were welcomed with a refreshing cocktail at reception and then taken to their room. Kate and Dick had arrived at heaven on earth! Dick had booked a water villa, which is a room built on stilts in the ocean with your very own entrance into the ocean. The deck at the back of the villa had a private Jacuzzi, whilst the front porch overlooked the extensive Indian Ocean. Meters and meters of clear, still, turquoise water with no sight of any other inhabitants or objects. The views were breath-taking and out of this world!

Kate was relieved and thrilled when she received her suit-case. Her mum certainly did an amazing job! She soon discovered that she had two outfits per day and plenty of shoes to match each outfit!

Kate and Dick spent seven nights on the island, most of which was spent sleeping, eating, snorkelling, swimming and chilling on the beach. Kate also learnt how to play table tennis for the first time. The number of times that they were intimate was far from what was expected when on honeymoon, she imagined. However, Kate still associated the discomfort of the actual act with the fact that she was new to this, and it would possibly get better as time went on.

The island was amazingly beautiful, and the couple were spoilt when it came to cuisines from around the world, freshly prepared three times a day. There was not a single thing that you could think of that was not there. The freshly squeezed fruit juices and fresh tropical fruits were refreshing and delicious! Kate's favourite drink was either the freshly squeezed pineapple or watermelon juice as she was still not allowed to drink an alcoholic beverage.

Most of the staff at the hotel thought that Kate and Dick were either British or from India. It is a common misperception by most abroad that South Africans are either African or

Caucasian. The other observation by most was that Kate and Dick really looked very young.

There is nothing more beautiful than the Indian Ocean boasting an average water temperature of 28°C. The calm turquoise water was where most of Kate and Dick's time were spent. Kate learnt how to snorkel for the first time and, because she was not a very strong swimmer, she had a life jacket on her which allowed her to just float and enjoy the marine life. Dick insisted on Kate holding his hand as he was afraid that she was not a very good swimmer and would stray away. The marine life was amazing. It was a snapshot of a scene from the movie, *Finding Nemo*. There were tons of angelfish, clown fish and all sorts of bright tropical fish in all sizes, shapes and colours at an arm's length away. It was unbelievable to think all this was possible to see just from snorkelling! It was absolutely picturesque!

On one of the days, Kate and Dick took a *Love Boat* cruise for the whole day which was lots of fun! They met an Italian couple that were also on their honeymoon and had just gotten married around the same time. One of the stops was a barren sandbar island in the middle of the ocean where guests could sunbath or swim. On the way back to the resort, Kate and Dick were fortunate to witness a pod of dolphins that swam beside the boat. As the boat boys whistled, the dolphins kept diving in and out of the water. Kate loved animals, and it was an absolute treat and beautiful scene to see dolphins in their natural habitat! It was a great day out cruising around the islands, meeting new people, swimming and snorkelling.

Every night after dinner, Kate and Dick would sit out with their legs hanging over the front porch dangling over the water. There was a large flood light which attracted many fish, including a large manta ray that visited!

During the day, there were often lemon sharks around the villas just outside the restaurant and guests would often feed them.

Kate and Dick both thoroughly enjoyed their honeymoon and first holiday away together. Kate, though, was not convinced that either of them felt that the honeymoon was the way they imagined it would turn out–especially the intimacy part! When the couple returned home, Dick shared his concerns about their intimacy. At the same time, Kate did not feel comfortable with the act at all. Kate always assigned the discomfort to it being new and something that would improve with time.

CHAPTER 5
Life in Bermuda

The following year, Kate and Dick moved to Bermuda on a two-year work contract. Although Kate was close to her family and she would have preferred to remain in South Africa; she felt that moving to a foreign country would give her and Dick the best chance! Kate believed that in the early stages of their marriage, it would be beneficial to ensure that they eliminated the family interference as much as possible.

The eight months post the wedding was difficult as entire weekends were spent at family due to the anticipation of the couple leaving the country. Kate's mum was not restrictive when it came to the amount of time Kate and Dick spent with the family. On the contrary, Dick's mom would stipulate that family lunches were strictly on a Saturday at noon. They had to be present and spend the entire day until the evening. As such, Kate felt it was only fair to do the same with her family on the Sunday and so, as a result, the whole weekend would be spent visiting family leaving Kate and Dick with little time to themselves.

After Dick's job was confirmed at an accounting firm, the agent managed to secure a job for Kate at a local pharmacy in the heart of Hamilton. Bermuda was an extremely small island, with only one hospital, a chain of pharmacies and Hamilton pharmacy. It was confirmed that Kate and Dick's work permits were arranged, and so they left South Africa on the 12th January 2007. Dick was due to start his new job on the Monday.

Kate and Dick's families were incredibly sad to bid them farewell. Bermuda was the furthest country on the globe from South Africa in terms of distance and time! There were no direct flights; the route is either via the UK or through the US. Kate and Dick opted to fly through the UK, as Kate had family in the UK that they could spend time with during the layover and change in airports. All the couple packed with them were their clothes. A new life was to be set up once they arrived.

As the plane touched down, either side of the runway was encircled with turquoise waters, this time the Atlantic Ocean. The couple arrived in Bermuda on the Sunday morning and were welcomed to the cheerful sounds of a Bermudian playing a piano.

As the couple made their way to the immigration counter, Kate discovered that her work permit was not available, and there was no record of the details that she was told to present upon arrival. Therefore, Kate had to enter the country on a visitor permit. On the other hand, all was in order with Dick's permit.

Once their bags were collected, they took a taxi to the apartment that they were to stay in for a month before finding their own place. The self-catering apartment was called the Parquet. The apartment resembled a hospital setting with extensive white floors and walls, and was very minimalistic in its decoration.

The misconception is that Bermuda is located within the Caribbean region. However, Bermuda is closer to countries on the east coast of the US. The average flying time to New York from Bermuda is approximately two hours. As such, the weather experienced in Bermuda is subtropical. December through to March is winter, in which very cool temperatures are experienced, lots of rain and gale-force winds.

Kate and Dick had a bit of sunshine on the Sunday, and so made the best of having lunch and then taking a walk down to Elbow Beach.

The beaches in Bermuda are beautiful and are often described as pink beaches. The white-coloured beach sand is speckled with finely pulverised remains of calcium carbonate shells and skeletons of invertebrates such as corals, forams, shells and clams. Foraminifera, in particular, homotrema rubrum, also known as forams, which are dark red skeletal animals, grow in large quantities on the underside of Bermuda's coral reefs. When the red forams die, the skeletons drop to the ocean floor. Wave action then erodes the forams. The skeletons become mixed with other debris on the seabed such as clams, snails and sea urchins. It is during this time that Bermuda's white sandy beaches take on their characteristic pink hue.

Another distinct visual characteristic that stands out is Bermuda's white limestone roof buildings, which are not just artistically impressive, but are used functionally due to the scarcity of fresh water on the island. The roofs are fashioned in a step-like slope with side gutters that funnel rainwater toward pipes leading into an underground tank, and form the main water source for bathing, cooking etc. Bottled water is consumed for drinking.

Modern exploration has discovered more efficient processes such as reverse osmosis. However, these plants supply mainly the larger hotels on the island. Most residents still depend upon their roofs for their water. On average, more than fifty percent of all portable water consumed in Bermuda comes from the roofs!

The water supply was certainly the most difficult to come to terms with for Kate. How could an island surrounded by gallons of water not have sufficient means to develop water infrastructure to supply fresh water to everyone?! This was a constant concern from Kate and Dick's landlords later when they moved into their apartment. The landlords did not want to rely on purchasing water from portal water tanks which were of lower quality and, as a result, were very strict on the consumption of water. This did not help and added to Dick's controlling character, that resulted in "if it's yellow, let it mellow, if it's brown flush it down". This became routine when the couple did not have guests!

Kate always enjoyed showering twice a day especially in summer, and she was particularly fond of standing under the flowing water. In the case of Bermuda, it was extremely humid, and your skin would constantly have a layer of sweat on it! Unfortunately, due to the water restrictions, Kate's enjoyable showers were a distant memory and the tap often had to be turned off during the soaping of her body and shampooing of her hair. It was a horrible feeling to constantly be stressed about the amount of water one was consuming.

Grocery shopping was interesting and difficult at the same time. Kate needed to decide on what brands of food and cleaning items she would pick. The quality of food was not the same as South Africa. Chicken often had a very dull greyish colour to it versus the bright white shimmer one would expect. Seafood and fish always seemed a better option. Fresh high-quality produce was also difficult to source, and most of the goods were imported from the US. Kate and Dick became accustomed to Canadian-style red-skinned potatoes and red-skinned onions instead of the usual white potatoes and onions. Groceries were packed into brown paper bags just as Kate had seen in the movies. Not long after they arrived in Bermuda, Kate asked her parents to ship them non-perishable goods so that they could at least enjoy their favourite biscuits and other luxuries from home that they could not substitute. Restaurants and eating out were quite expensive and became a treat as opposed to something that they did often.

It was the simple necessities such as food, water and standard of living that made Kate miss home so terribly!

Dick left to his first day of work on the Monday morning, and Kate had an entire day to unpack their suitcases. By mid-day, she was bored and felt cooped up in the apartment whilst it was raining outside. She followed up with the pharmacy and found out that there was a delay in her work permit. The Pharmacy Council in Bermuda had set meetings at which they would discuss new pharmacists. Her work permit application could not be completed as it was the first time that they had a South African pharmacist on the island. They needed to send away her original degree certificate and university results to the UK for them to be authenticated against international requirements. Since no one had communicated this to Kate prior to her arrival, she did not have the original documents with her and had to have them posted. Also, once the documents were received, it was not guaranteed that they would be reviewed immediately as this was only done at scheduled or planned council meetings. As a result, Kate sat at home not knowing a soul. The dark and dreary weather outside did not help either, and Kate was left with a limited number of cable TV channels available to watch. Moreover, anyone that knew Kate well understood that she was not a TV person, but rather enjoyed the interaction and personal contact with people.

A few days later, Kate decided to visit the pharmacy and met Andrea, who later became a dear friend. Andrea was from Jamaica, as was Shannon. Andrea immediately welcomed Kate with a warm and caring disposition. They instantly hit it off and started chatting. Andrea offered to assist Kate in any way that she needed both on a professional and personal level. Whilst they were getting acquainted, a short, sturdy, dark-haired woman with glasses approached the two ladies all flustered and slightly red in the face and introduced herself as Lynn, Kate's new boss!

Lynn seemed uncomfortable and possibly felt insecure that Kate was speaking to Andrea and not her. This of course was not the ladies' intention, but they were sure to look out for it when Kate finally arrived at work. Andrea kindly shared study notes with Kate and offered to tutor her during her spare time. This would make use of any free time and ensure that Kate was ready in the following three months to take the exam to be allowed to work as a pharmacist in Bermuda.

Andrea was dating a fellow African from Uganda, and they were engaged in July later that year. These were the only friends that Kate made from work. Later that year, they were happy to celebrate when Kate passed her Bermudian exam thanks to Andrea's support and assistance.

Kate and Dick were invited to Dick's boss' home, also a South African who held a dinner at his place to welcome all the newcomers to their firm. Kate and Dick shared a taxi with a

German couple that were also staying at the Parquet. They had a three-month old new-born baby. Kate always admired their spirit and endurance, making a big move to a foreign country with such a small baby! They immediately connected with them and became very close friends. Taryn was a stay-at-home mum, and so Kate enjoyed her company whilst still at home waiting for her work permit to be issued. Once the first month was over, both families moved to opposite ends of the island, but it was a relatively short distance to see each other.

The most common and economical mode of transport on the island was a moped motorbike. Once Dick got to work and was settled, he had to go and apply for his license. He purchased a moped. Kate struggled to handle the moped given her tiny frame, let alone the gale force winds and rain! They used the moped for a few months before Kate had to ask her dad to kindly assist her in getting a car, rather! Kate was used to the luxury of a car. Besides, it was just easier that way transporting groceries, not getting wet and buying bigger items for the house.

A month later, Kate and Dick moved into an apartment that they found close to Hamilton. This was convenient for them as they both worked close by. It was the only time that they had the luxury of the least amount of traffic to work. Bermuda was by far the most relaxing in terms of the amount of time that you had to sleep and do your own activities besides the normal day-to-day chores or work. Kate and Dick had to adjust to cleaning their apartment on their own, as it was very expensive to get a routine helper.

It was extremely stressful having to set up house again as Dick was the only earner for the first four months of the year. The apartment was furnished with the basics, but since the couple only took their clothes with them, they had to buy all other essential items such as crockery, towels and linen. During this time, Dick did not stop supporting his family back home and always ensured that he still sent money home to help his mom without omitting a month. Kate was not sure whether his family were fully aware of their circumstances and whether they truly appreciated the sacrifice and their efforts.

Kate didn't have any issues with her teeth prior to moving to Bermuda but suffered with an extreme toothache not long after they arrived. Kate had to find a dentist who, after consultation, informed her that one of her wisdom teeth had come out and needed to be removed. In the chair right there, he gave her some anaesthetic and began working. Kate did not mind; she was a strong girl and could tolerate great levels of pain! Well, this was short-lived as she began to feel extreme pain as he struggled to remove the tooth. It felt like her jaw was going to break. Once she started to feel the warm blood trickle down her cheek, she started to cry! It was a horrifying experience that she did not wish to re-live! Thankfully, Kate's other wisdom teeth were intact, and the dentist did not need to touch any of them. Her cheeks were severely swollen making her face completely squared off, and it took her many days to recover.

Dick had taught Kate how to play Texas Hold'em poker before they left for Bermuda, and this fittingly was to become one of their hobbies and pastimes. Dick's closest friend was Andrew from Switzerland. He was dating a Swiss girl, Kelly, who had massive naturally big boobs! The couples would often hang out on the weekends together, barbeque and play poker. It was during this time that Kate had to address the issue of Dick not wanting her to drink any alcohol. Kate had grown up with her parents allowing her to drink alcohol in the safe environment of their home. Kate's dad bought ciders for the teenagers and allowed them to drink in his presence. It was done socially and not with the aim for anyone to get drunk. Kate explained this to Dick. Just because his dad was an alcoholic, it did not mean that everyone needed to be painted with the same brush. Dick finally agreed and allowed Kate to have the odd glass of champagne with their new friends.

Dick would buy lunch from a takeaway shop close by his office, and he made friends with a lovely Indian woman from Malaysia. She ran the Orient takeaway shop and worked at their sit-down restaurant further up in town. Her husband was a talented pastry chef and worked at one of the popular hotels on the island. The couple had been on the island for a good few years before Kate and Dick. It saddened Kate to know how many hours people in the food and service industry had to work in order to earn a decent salary. Whilst this was a good salary in comparison to their birth countries, they still did not earn nearly as much as the professionals on the island. Yet, the dollars earned were significant enough to allow for savings to send back home to their families.

Taryn was part of a ladies' club for stay-at-home women, and Kate joined her to pass some of her time. The first event that Kate joined was a golf day arranged for the ladies. Kate had not played golf before but quite enjoyed the swing motion and the pleasure of hitting the golf ball, when contact was made, that is! Kate also met a lovely South African woman, Joan, who happened to stay in the same suburb as Kate and Dick back in South Africa! Joan and her husband soon became Kate and Dick's parents away from home!

Apart from the delay to Kate starting work, missing family, feeling homesick and eating copious amounts of chocolate, Kate and Dick managed to make many new friends. This was a great support network when setting up in a foreign country. Bermudians are not very welcoming to expats as almost all the professional jobs – service and tourism industries included – are held by expats.

Bermuda is fifty-three point two square kilometres and the concept of Island Syndrome and the feeling of being restricted existed for sure. It only takes about forty minutes to drive from one end of the island to the other, and this is mainly due to the narrow and winding roads. The population size of Bermuda is approximately sixty-two thousand people. This was a contrast and big adjustment for Kate and Dick who were accustomed to living in a large city such as their hometown, Johannesburg. They would often see the same faces across the island when out and about. As such, people often go off the island just for a break. Unfortunately, Kate and Dick were not advised to apply for a US visa in South Africa before leaving the country, and they had to be a resident in Bermuda for one year first prior to being allowed to apply for a US visa. This was a huge setback as the couple could not leave the island and missed the opportunity to go away on weekends to the nearby neighbouring US states.

In April, the couple were fortunate that Dick had a week of work training in Montréal, Canada, and they had the opportunity of going off the island for the first time. Taryn, the baby and Kate joined their husbands, and had a wonderful week touring the city of Montréal. They walked the streets, ate the most amazing fresh bagels bursting with various flavours of cream cheese, and had many delicious dinners. It was extremely cold and even snowed whilst they visited. This was Dick's first experience of snow, and his colleagues took time during the day to have fun in the snow. They even built a snowman!

Kate and Dick's first year wedding anniversary fell in the same week that they were in Montréal. They agreed that they would go out alone for dinner that evening, just the two of them. They had gone shopping for gifts for each other earlier that week, so Kate was not expecting anything on the day. During the day, Kate would spend her time with Taryn and the baby. She would head back to their room when the men arrived back from the office. On this day, Kate was excited to get back to their room to take a shower and get ready for their anniversary dinner date. To her dismay, when Kate arrived back to the room, Dick and her got into an argument, because as she doublechecked the address of the restaurant that they were going to, she stumbled upon pornographic material on his laptop! She was broken! She immediately burst into tears and could not stop sobbing. She felt betrayed and felt as if she was just not good enough for him! Dick did not apologise to her nor console her. Dick justified his actions by saying that a man has needs, and he needed to satisfy his needs.

Kate eventually pulled herself together, and they got ready and went out for dinner. It was a vegetarian day, and so Dick chose a Thai restaurant which catered for vegetarians. The restaurant's speciality was incorporating tofu sculpted into various shapes such as prawns and chicken but prepared as a full vegetarian dish. The meals were every unique and nothing like they had eaten before.

Kate eventually started working after the couple returned from Montréal, almost four months after arriving on the island. Kate was thrilled to be back at work and occupied. This was her first job as a pharmacist, and she was enthusiastic and excited for what lay ahead.

Due to the large time difference between Bermuda and home, the couple only really spoke to family over the weekends. Once again, this was not a fair split. Dick and Kate always had to call his family, whereas Kate's family would always call them. Kate found it very difficult speaking to her family over the phone as she missed them terribly, especially at the onset with her struggle to settle in. These were the days just prior to the launch of the social media world – no facetiming and the couple would therefore also email as often as possible in-between, and exchange photos with updates of their new experiences. Kate's dad eventually started commenting about the weight she had gained, and suggested that Kate get to the gym or start doing something to be active! Dick of course loved these comments, but Kate was really upset with her dad's feedback! Her dad was, in a way, accurate as she eventually tried on an outfit that she wanted to wear for the first day of work, and the zip on the pants would not close! This was all a little strange for Kate as she was always underweight. The staple diet of two Kit Kat Chunkies and half a slab of whole nut chocolate a day for the past four months had caught up with Kate sitting at home!

It was a Sunday and Mother's Day in South Africa. Kate and Dick had gone out for the day to friends. When they got back home, Kate's mum had called to say that Dick's sister's boyfriend had been in a car accident and was in a critical state in the intensive care unit at the hospital. It was a few days later that he passed away at the young age of twenty-one. Kate and Dick arranged to go back home to see his sister. However, they did not make it in time for the funeral due to the long travelling time.

Kate really felt incredibly sad for Dick's sister. They were never close, but Kate felt that the passing of her boyfriend brought them a little closer. Kate empathised with her in some ways because this was her first serious boyfriend, and Kate identified with that. Kate remembered what it was like when she broke up with her first boyfriend, and although he did not pass away, the suddenness and unexpectedness made it feel like he was dead to her at the time. During the time that they were at the funeral house, there was a woman doing palm readings. Everyone was doing it, and so Kate waited for a turn. The lady looked at her palm and said that she had two major dark lines, which were representative of two significant relationships in her life. Both were relationships that were not going to last for this lifetime. As she said this, she realised where this was going and with awkwardness ended the reading. This always played at the back of Kate's mind because the second significant relationship was the one she was currently in with Dick. They spent a week in South Africa, and it was great seeing all of their family again before returning to Bermuda.

The couple felt very unsettled on their return. Kate started work and had many difficult days. Lynn had to sign off on every prescription that she dispensed. Kate was required to work as an intern under Lynn's supervision for three weeks. Lynn made no attempt to mentor or teach Kate but seemed as though she was waiting for Kate to make mistakes and then make a big deal out of it. Andrea was always around to support Kate, but because they worked shifts between the four pharmacists, Kate could not avoid working with Lynn alone.

Kate found the patients to be difficult, and it was challenging for her to understand the Bermudian accent, which was a mixture of a Caribbean and an American accent. The experience was great for Kate, as all the medication was imported from Canada and the UK. Therefore, she had to learn trade names of products from these countries. In addition, the pharmacist is given more prescribing power in relation to the over-the-counter products and, as such, patients would come in to ask for advice and a suitable treatment.

Kate's greatest learning came from her relationship with Lynn; it was her first working relationship, and she felt very patronised by Lynn. She was miserable at work, besides not enjoying the people and the work itself. Her strained relationship with Lynn made it more difficult. Kate's confidence was very low, and she just wanted to stop and to go back home. She would cry every day and hated going to work. Andrea would try to encourage her, and assisted her in seeing things from different perspectives, but Kate wanted nothing more than to go back home.

Kate and Dick joined the Bermuda Poker tour, which was a weekly cash game with a buy-in of $40. Kate initially did not want to play as she was afraid that she would not be good at it, but eventually Dick and the event organiser convinced her. Moreover, what do you know, it ended up being great , and Kate made it to the top 10 of the female league! Unfortunately for Kate and Dick, there was a dispute on the island as to whether the cash poker games were legal, and the league was soon cancelled.

Andrew bought a boat, and it became a great pastime to go out onto the ocean. In summer, the sun would only set much later in the evening, at around 8pm, and so they would have a good few hours after work to go out and enjoy the waters. Andrew did wakeboarding. Wakeboarding is a surface water sport which entails riding on a wakeboard on the surface of the water. The wakeboard is a wide board resembling a surfboard but with shoe-like mountings on it. The rider is towed behind a motorboat typically at speeds averaging between 30-40 km/hr depending on the board size, rider's weight and skill level. Dick and Andrew spent much of their spare time wakeboarding whilst Kate would often enjoy driving the boat and taking videos and photos of them. At that stage, Kate was not even going to attempt wakeboarding, which requires a great deal of upper body and core strength to lift yourself out of the wake formed behind the boat.

Summer in Bermuda is extremely humid. Humidity levels can reach ninety-five percent and above. To Kate and Dick's astonishment, they learnt that mould grows on leather shoes and belts due to the high humidity. Air conditioning units alone were not enough, a dehumidifier was required to remove the water content from the air to keep the room dry. To Kate's disappointment, she had to throw away her favourite pair of leather sandals that were covered in a thick layer of green mould by the time summer arrived when she had unpacked them to wear! Clothes could not be air-dried outside on a washing line, and so all clothing had to go into the tumble dryer.

Bermuda boasts the highest concentration of golf courses per square mile in the world! There are nine amazing golf courses with spectacular scenery and views of the island. Dick grew up playing golf but did not really spend much time playing the sport in his later years. It was therefore appropriate for Kate to learn to play golf! Dick taught her the basics, and it was best to then move onto the lessons provided by the women's club for both his and her sanity! Kate and Dick went to the driving range at least twice a week, and Kate played on a nine-hole course for the first time!

Taryn and her husband left the island in July of 2007, and whilst this was the best option for their family, it was very sad for Kate and Dick. Kelly had broken up with Andrew and started dating a South African man that worked on the same team as Andrew and Dick! This was discouraging as most of the friends seemed to be going through a slump.

Kate felt all perspectives of life in Bermuda to be trying. Apart from the amazing friendships that were created and having so much free time on hand, she struggled with the other aspects. As the sixth month at Hamilton Pharmacy approached, Kate chatted to her parents and Dick to decide what was best for her work. Kate and Dick eventually made the decision after her parents had visited in the summer that she would resign, and they would return home in December. As it was still within the first six months of her contract, she could leave with immediate effect. She did not have to work until December when the couple planned to leave the island.

Dick's work, on the other hand, was going very well. He was even offered another position at a re-insurance firm, and they were willing to pay him enough that Kate could stay at home. No amount of dollars in the world would make Kate happy at this stage.

Since Dick's work was going considerably well and he did not mind staying out the two years, Kate felt bad that she put a damper on things. Dick, however, did find it more difficult being away from home after his sister's boyfriend's death, and agreed that it was best for them to return home. Dick had to break his contract, but they were extremely fortunate that they could afford to pay back what they owed the company to return to South Africa.

The night that the plane took off into the sky, Kate burst out crying! It was a feeling of relief to finally be able to escape the adversities that she had experienced over the last eleven months.

CHAPTER 6
I Am Going Home

Kate and Dick spent two weeks in London en route home as Dick had never been to London before. They enjoyed the time sightseeing with Kate's cousins, but could not wait to get home! Kate and Dick almost missed their flight leaving London. They had misjudged the traffic to the airport after dinner, and their boarding gate, of course, was right at the end. Never had they run so fast to make sure that they reached the gate on time to board the plane home!

Their immediate families were all at the airport to welcome the couple home! Everyone was thrilled to have them back! Before they reached home, Dick had already mentioned to Kate that as soon as they got home, they would have to stay with his mom and sister first. His sister was going through a difficult time, still grieving the loss of her boyfriend. So straight from the airport, they all went to Dick's house. The first few days were good to be back in South Africa. Not long after they arrived, one of Kate's cousins turned twenty-one. Because Kate and Dick were staying with his mom at the time, Dick's mom and sister were invited to the party as well. At the party, Dick's sister seemed to have hit it off with two of Kate's cousins. In the next day or two, Kate's cousins were coming to the house to fetch Dick's sister to go out clubbing. Kate could anticipate a disastrous outcome to this newfound 'friendship' that was blossoming! On one occasion, Kate's cousin offered to take her shopping as Dick was not keen, and Dick's sister joined too. During this outing, Kate could tell that Dick's sister was only using him to drive her around to go out clubbing at night. It was convenient and safe as they both lived close by in the same area in the south of Joburg. Kate then met her cousin alone the day after, and begged him to please stay away from Dick's sister. She knew that he did not live up to her taste or expectations in guys and was merely using him to drive her around. He insisted that she was flirting with him and believed that there was more to it.

Not long after this, Dick confronted Kate, saying that her cousin and his sister had a falling-out and he called her ugly names. Kate was extremely upset and told Dick that she did not want to get involved because when things were going well, she was not a part of anything, and now because things turned for the worst, it was because of her cousin! Dick threatened Kate, and said that he and his brother would physically harm her cousin because of the name calling and the fact that he hurt their sister. After this incident, family functions were very awkward as Dick, his mother and sister would ignore Kate's two cousins.

Kate and Dick then went and stayed with her parents for a while before they had to find an apartment of their own. It was during this time that Kate locumed at the nearby pharmacy for a month. Dick continued finishing off his contract with Bermuda by working remotely from South Africa.

It was in February that Dick started working at an auditing firm in South Africa, and in March that Kate started working at a local pharmaceutical manufacturer.

Kate and Dick agreed that they would find an apartment in the Lonehill area. This is where they stayed after they got married before moving to Bermuda, and they quite enjoyed the area. They found a new development and were thrilled with the apartment. The day that they took their parents to see the apartment, Dick's mom complained that it was too small for the price being asked!

In June 2008, Kate and Dick attended a wedding of a close family friend. Kate and the bride grew up together and shared many childhood memories before Kate's family migrated to

Australia. After the wedding, Kate's sister and brother-in-law planned a family vacation for a week. During the second last evening, whilst they were all playing board games, an argument occurred between Kate's sister and Dick! Dick was being his usual self, speaking down on Kate, and mocking her if she did not get the answers correct and in time. Kate's sister eventually lashed out and cursed at Dick! Kate's parents and everyone else were just shocked! Dick was angry again, and he felt that Kate or her parents should have said something to her sister, but they did not. Needless to say, the trip home was extremely long and painful. Upon arriving back in Joburg, Kate and Dick were to move into their new apartment. Dick was still really upset with Kate's sister. Kate found the position awkward again. She understood why her sister behaved in that way; however, she wished she would have told Dick that his behaviour was unreasonable in a more polite way.

Kate and her sister always had major sibling rivalry between them. There was almost an eight-year age gap between them. Kate's dad had only planned to have the one child, but Kate's mum felt that her sister was extremely spoilt, being the only grandchild and niece in the family. As a result, Kate arrived many years later. Although the two girls were both brought up in the same household, under the same roof, by the same parents and afforded the same opportunities in life, they were contrastingly different. Kate believes that this was because of very different choices made by the two.

Kate's sister never really liked Dick from the start and felt that he changed Kate. There were no valid reasons for not liking him, but Kate believes that the sibling rivalry was just transferred to him as well, naturally him being her spouse. In a world consumed by status and ego, the fact that they were a highly successful couple did not make it any easier.

Kate and Dick soon settled into their first-owned apartment! The routine began again with family lunches on the weekend and no time for the couple.

Kate and Dick were struggling over two years into the marriage to connect. The first year was extremely difficult with the adjustment of living together and getting into a routine. The second year in Bermuda had its own set of challenges, working and living in a foreign country. Returning home seemed to make no difference, the couple were always fighting and could not see eye to eye. Kate and Dick had been for marriage counselling before they got married, and so they decided to try it out again. This time, they saw a different therapist.

Kate and Dick were ashamed, and so they did not tell any of their family that they were going for counselling. The lady gave them some valuable exercises to do, and practices that could be applied daily to their circumstances. For example, after a fight, Dick would never want to sit and talk about it. Therefore, they had to agree on a time out period for him, after which he had to discuss the issue with Kate. The therapist also introduced the couple to the book called *The Five Love Languages* by Gary Chapman. It was during counselling that Dick raised their intimacy issues. The therapist suggested that they see a sex therapist, but also went on to mention something Kate would not forget. She said that Kate would have no issues and would be swinging from the chandeliers with the next person! Kate was obliging and was willing to see a sex therapist if intimacy was important to him and critical to their relationship. However, to Kate's surprise, Dick refused to see a sex therapist and said that they needed to sort the issue out on their own.

The struggles in their relationship and marriage continued, and at least once a year Dick would bring up the intimacy issues. Kate really did try her best in this department, but was lost as to how to fix it, and it always appeared the blame was on her.

CHAPTER 7
Around The World

Kate and Dick were fortunate to travel at least once a year to different destinations around the world. They planned their trips around their wedding anniversary and would tend to go away then.

Besides Kate and Dick's honeymoon, and their revisit to the Maldives for their five-year wedding anniversary, the holiday that stood out the most for Kate was the trip that they took in 2012.

In 2012, Kate and Dick decided that this would be their last holiday together before starting a family. They planned a three-week long summer holiday to the United States. This was by far the most memorable trip Kate experienced with Dick. In April, for their wedding anniversary, Dick was away traveling on business, so he wrote Kate the following:

"Happy 6th Anniversary my Angel

What an amazing 6 years it has been. I am more in love with you now than the day we first met, our 1st anniversary, your 21st birthday, our registration, our wedding or any previous time!

We have GROWN together, in numerous ways and forms. Every day our marriage and bond get stronger and stronger, and it will continue to grow. My love for you is deep, and my heart is so content with the knowledge that you are mine. I have truly hit the jackpot having you as mine and being this lucky is something few people will ever know in a lifetime.

I can't wait for our trip to the States to celebrate our Anniversary. I am really sad that I could not be with you on our special day. There's a surprise I was hoping to give you as your birthday/anniversary gift which unfortunately has not panned out. Let me now tell you what it is:

The reason I was delaying on the Miami accommodation and bookings was because I wanted to surprise you by taking you to Los Angeles. For what? To see Ellen of course! I was checking her website every day for tickets and unfortunately to my dismay, her season has come to an end and they are not shooting any shows from June until August (announced two weeks ago on the website). They will only return in September! This was really sad for me, and I'm really sorry you couldn't experience this! Maybe one day later, hopefully if she's still on TV. The following is an e-mail (limit of 1500 words) I mailed on her website before I knew that tickets are free, and you just need to check online. Unfortunately, I have not received a response from the show. I e-mailed twice to make sure:

'Dear Ellen,

This is my most important e-mail ever. I am Dickxxxxxxx (Johannesburg, South Africa) & writing in the hope that you can help me give my wife the greatest gift: to see You in person. In 2007, our second year of marriage, my wife and I went on working permits to Bermuda. We both had jobs but a delay in her work permit resulted in her being without work for four months. Far away from home and alone, she went through depression ,crying every day & wanted to return. Whenever she spoke to family, she would breakdown and cry. Then came YOU! While sitting at home she discovered your show, counting down the hours every day. You put the biggest smile on her face, and I can't tell you how much I'm indebted to you for this. You are the reason my wife got through the depression. My wife is not one for idolising celebrities. However, there are two people she adores, You & Céline Dion. We are fortunate enough that she will realise one of her dreams, seeing Céline live in Vegas. She turns 30 this year and is studying her MBA part-time while working, so most of her free time is taken by studies. This is our last trip before we plan for our first child, and her final MBA year. I love her dearly & there's no greater gift I can give her than to see you. All I'm asking for is to get tickets for the show for the only dates I can take her (14 or 15 June). We are due in Miami after Vegas, but I would like to make a SURPRISE detour via the Ellen Show. Being from South Africa, this is the only chance I will have to do this for her.'

I love you so much and I miss you even more!

Happy Anniversary my angel!"

Kate and Dick flew directly into New York and arrived bright and early in the morning. They hit the ground running and immediately took an hour-long bus ride to the largest outlet mall in New York. With two empty suitcases to fill, this was complete heaven for Kate! They went to all of her favourite stores, and Kate shopped to her heart's content! The next day, Kate and Dick started out early in the morning and took the hop-on hop-off bus, which was the easiest way to get around the big apple and to be able to see all the main attractions. It was a jam-packed full four days of sightseeing. Kate and Dick went to Central Park, Grand Central Station, The Statue of Liberty, Staten Island, Brooklyn Bridge, The Empire State building, Times Square, Rockefeller Centre, Chinatown, Little Italy, The World Trade Centre, and finally, Yankee Stadium. They watched the New York Yankees play at their home ground. They also fit in a ferry ride to Hoboken to visit Carlo's Bakery! New York is an amazing city that does not go to sleep and lives up to everything one sees in the movies! There was an incredible buzz and a continuous fast pace, where everyone around you seemed to be on the run. The standard city block in Manhattan is about eighty by two hundred and seventy-four meters, and together the blocks form a giant grid. In New York, the difference between streets and avenues is critical, and definitely something to bear in mind whilst walking! The most basic thing to remember is that the avenues run north and south, whilst the streets run east and west. Although Kate and Dick had Google maps on their phones to navigate, they did run into a few instances in which they were completely lost and walking in the wrong direction!

Kate and Dick's next stop was Las Vegas! As you arrive at the airport, the ka-ching sound greets you as the arrival hallways are filled with slot machines! Welcome to Sin City! The hotels in Vegas are striking and spectacular! Kate and Dick had a luxurious, opulent suite at the Venetian hotel, and were convinced that this room could have been issued in error!

Kate and Dick watched fantastic live shows, such as the Phantom of the Opera, Cirque du Soleil, The Blue Man Group and her absolute dream come true – Céline Dion at The Colosseum! The Colosseum has a very intimate setting. Kate had goose bumps from the moment the show began! It was a theatrical performance not only because of Céline's amazing voice, but also because of the stage set up, costumes and choreography. Kate was absolutely honoured to have received such a beautiful gift to see her favourite music artist, and in such an exclusive setting!

Kate convinced Dick to go out to a nightclub one evening in Vegas. Again, the experience was nothing like she had seen before. The nightclub was situated at the poolside of one of the hotel properties on the Vegas strip. There were many VIP seating booths and seated areas outside with the dance floor inside. A good night out is always heightened with great music! One of the DJs that played that evening was Skrillex, who later became incredibly famous around the world!

The Stratosphere is a hotel in Vegas, and the property's main attraction is the three hundred and fifty metre Stratosphere Tower which is the second tallest tower in the Western Hemisphere and houses three major thrill rides, Big Shot, Insanity and X Scream.

Big Shot shoots you vertically one hundred and sixty feet up into the air at forty-five miles per hour as you overlook the majestic Las Vegas valley. In a matter of seconds, the ride catapults sixteen riders from the nine hundred- and twenty-one-foot-high platform up the Tower's mast to a height of one thousand and eighty-one feet and down again. Just as you are about to catch your breath, you will be shot up again!

Insanity is a massive metal mechanical arm that extends out sixty-four feet over the edge of the Stratosphere tower at a height of over nine hundred feet. Riders are propelled at an angle of seventy degrees, which tilts your body into one position and then back straight down. If you are brave enough to keep your eyes open, you are offered the breath-taking view of the historic downtown of old Las Vegas.

X Scream propels riders headfirst, twenty-seven feet over the edge of The Stratosphere. After being shot over the edge, you dangle weightlessly above the famous Las Vegas strip before being pulled back and propelled over again for more.

Kate thoroughly enjoyed these crazy rides, being the adrenaline junkie that she was! Dick, on the hand, was petrified and refused to go on any for a second round!

Kate and Dick spent their next few nights at the Bellagio Hotel. The entrance of the hotel has a ceiling that is covered with Chihuly's art blossoms, Fiori di Como – a glass sculpture of delicate flowers created in a rainbow of bright colours. The couple had an amazing room that overlooked the Bellagio fountains. Inspired by the Lake Como town of Bellagio in Italy, the hotel boasts an eight-acre lake between the hotel building and the Vegas Strip which houses the fountains. There are magnificent aquatic shows which are choreographed with music and lights. Each day ended on a high with the curtains drawn back, and Kate and Dick watching the glorious body of water that danced to the music so eloquently.

Kate and Dick's trip was planned at the same time as the World Series of Poker. Dick had been following poker on TV prior to them leaving Bermuda, so they were delighted to go and watch the famous poker players from around the world. Dick was fortunate enough to meet his all-time favourite Canadian poker player, Daniel Negreanu! Other famous players seen were Phil Ivey, Phil Hellmuth and Victor Ramdin, to name but a few. It was a tremendous experience being just a few feet away from the table and being able to watch them play live!

Kate and Dick took a sunset helicopter ride into the Grand Canyon, which was absolutely breath-taking, unfathomable and very picturesque! The Grand Canyon is extremely large and is considered four times as big as Los Angeles. The top of the canyon is rather flat and drops down into the rugged elements below. It has various layers of reds, yellows, ochres and orange hues seemingly painted over strangely shaped rock formations and broken cliffs. There are no words that would do justice to describe this wonder of the world, which Kate and Dick were so blessed to see!

They stayed in the most beautiful hotels in Vegas and found themselves at times in surroundings just short of pure bliss and romance. None of this, however, seemed to assist in igniting any fire between them.

Kate and Dick's next stop was Miami. They had a short but memorable time in Miami, using a Segway to tour South Beach and having a fun-filled evening at Mangos, which hosts cabaret shows, fine cuisine, live bands and DJs. They also had the pleasure of spending some time with close family friends in West Palm Beach.

Kate and Dick then took a seven-night Caribbean cruise from Fort Lauderdale near Miami. The Royal Caribbean Allure of the Seas, at the time, was the largest passenger ship carrying five thousand four hundred and ninety-two passengers at double occupancy or six thousand four hundred and fifty-two when every compartment is full.

On deck, one could never find yourself being bored, with an extensive entertainment line-up, including an indoor ice-skating rink, various clubs, restaurants, lounges, theatres and casinos. The Royal Promenade is the signature shopping area extending the length of a football field. The outdoor Boardwalk theme was inspired by Coney Island and was filled with many restaurants, shops, a carousel for the kids and Aqua Theatre. There is even a Central Park on board! There was an entire deck dedicated to kids and Adventure Ocean which includes a FlowRider Surf Simulator, a zipline, mini-golf, ping-pong tables and basketball courts.

The cruise liner had three stops at the following ports: Haiti, Falmouth (Jamaica) and Cozumel (Mexico).

Haiti was fun-filled with jet skis and a zipline that extended down from the highest point to the beach.

Jamaica was memorable as Kate had her first experience of swimming with dolphins! Kate always loved dolphins growing up and, although she had the opportunity to touch them in Bermuda, this was a unique experience, being completely free to swim with them. Dolphins have an exceptionally smooth, sleek, completely hairless but rubbery texture to their skin. It was an utterly amazing encounter for Kate! Kate and Dick also visited the Dunn's River waterfalls which they walked up and swam down. It was loads of fun!

In Cozumel, Kate and Dick attended a Salsa course that was two-fold: how to make salsa and how to dance the salsa! They also went shopping for her 30th birthday gift from Dick which was a white gold diamond jewellery set!

Kate and Dick's US summer vacation was by far the most memorable experience they shared and will always be treasured by Kate!

CHAPTER 8
Perfectly Imperfect

Jane was not too far off when she thought that Kate and Dick would make a good match … many people that saw the couple together, especially in the early days, thought they were a match made in heaven! Kate and Dick looked good together, matched well on paper and seemed to have everything under control; bills were paid on time, and they were completely independent of family when it came to finances.

When Kate and Dick first started dating, strangers would comment and say that they looked like brother and sister! This happened on more than three occasions! It was somewhat odd, because if strangers saw Dick, his sister and Kate together, they would automatically guess that Dick and his sister were in a relationship and that Kate was Dick's sister instead.

Kate and Dick made a perfect team and were highly successful in the material element of things. They matched in that they were both resourceful people and achieved whatever they set their minds on. They had similar taste when it came to the furnishing of their house and first apartment, which was extremely comfortable, brand-new and in a quaint little suburb. When it came to electronic equipment, Dick made sure he always had the best! Kate was only allowed to drive a Honda make of car, as Dick was a Honda fanatic and, as such, dictated that their cars were only allowed to be of that make.

Because Dick and Kate were both virgins when they got married, they spent some time talking about the anticipation that lay ahead. They shared their excitement about the intimacy they would eventually experience when they would be married. Kate imagined a lot of exploring, the discovery of sharing a special intimate connection, and a significant desire to be with the one she loved. However, this sadly was not the case. Kate and Dick's honeymoon was no different. In the early stage of their marriage, Kate recalled an intimate moment in which she felt uncomfortable as the whole experience was feeling claustrophobic and forced. She tried her best to continue, though without saying anything to Dick. Dick continued and they went all the way through, and, at the end, he said to Kate that it felt as though he was violating her and would therefore never initiate intimate moments again. Going forward, this would be her job!

Kate was shocked, scared and really did not know what to do or say or how to approach the topic. Kate found it difficult to initiate these intimate moments. She would try various techniques from organising dinners with candles to create a romantic ambiance, to buying games that could be fun to get things spiced up in the bedroom. Kate even suggested going to an event called Sexpo, an exhibition of all things to do with sex!

Kate eventually gave up and let it be as she did not know how this could be improved. Her suggestions were always shot down when it came to ways to change things up. Kate and Dick could easily go for weeks, sometimes even a month, without any intimacy.

Dick perceived Kate as a nun and a prude, and would often tell this to their friends when naughty conversations came up. Kate would cringe listening to him and would be embarrassed thinking that he did not even know who she truly was. When *Fifty Shades of Grey* launched and everyone was talking about it, Dick would say to friends, "Do you know who my wife is? She would not read the books nor watch the movie". When the movie came out, Kate did however take pleasure in watching it on night out with her girlfriends!

Early on in their relationship, it was exceedingly difficult for Kate to voice how she felt about Dick's family and their actions. Dick would automatically become defensive, and they would fight about it. Kate chose not to point anything out to him and hoped, rather, that he would eventually see it all for himself.

Kate and Dick's marriage was extremely structured, and Kate really craved spontaneity. Although Kate enjoyed planning as much as possible, she also enjoyed being carefree, adventurous and spontaneous. For example, she would have liked to get up on a Sunday morning and take a drive to a beautiful spot in nature for a picnic.

Since their Saturdays were filled with the family visits, Kate and Dick were only really left with a Friday evening or Sunday. On Friday evenings, they enjoyed spending time with friends or Kate would go out for a girl's night. Most Sundays were the routine car wash ritual (where conversations were still limited), out for lunch and then a movie at home or at the cinema. If Dick did not enjoy the company of Kate's family or friends, he would not spend time with them. This, of course, made it difficult for Kate when they were invited out, and she had to decline or come up with an excuse.

Dick had control of all aspects at home, including deciding the amount of monthly spending money they should have, and telling her how he thought she should do things in the kitchen when preparing meals! This would really annoy Kate due to the way in which Dick would share his thoughts and opinions. It was never in a loving and suggesting manner, but rather authoritative. Every weekday evening before bed, Kate had to take out the clothes that she would be wearing the next day so that he could iron them. Kate longed for Dick to be her partner and equal rather than an authoritarian figure.

Dick's best friend would often comment about how lucky Dick was to have Kate in his life, and that one day Kate would get fed up with him and possibly smack him! Well, this never happened, of course, as Kate was patient and tolerant, whilst her true emotions would stew beneath the surface!

Kate and Dick spent a lot of time with Dick's uncle (his mom's brother). Kate met him, his wife and only daughter initially during Dick's brother's wedding but did not really get close to them. A few years later, Kate and Dick ended up spending lots of time with them when they would travel up to Johannesburg to visit. It was during this time that Kate discovered that they knew what Dick's mother was all about. They were extremely supportive of Kate and Dick's marriage, and they really enjoyed spending time with them. During one of their visits, Kate was so embarrassed when Dick called her a bitch in front of his uncle and his family. Kate was ashamed and could not believe that he would say this in front of them no matter how upset he was with her. This was not the only time that he used the term to describe Kate. He also did it in front of her cousins on one occasion. On each occasion, no one said anything, but it really made Kate feel humiliated and hurt as there was no reason to use this degrading term in front of people.

Kate and Dick lived in their first apartment for six years, and then started looking at purchasing a free-standing house. They first started looking in the same suburb. However, free-standing houses were rare, as apartments were more pre-dominant in the area. Then, they decided to branch out and look in the neighbouring suburb.

Kate and Dick were viewing a few houses, but there was always something that was missing or not as they wished. It was just before her mum's sixtieth birthday, whilst her UK family were visiting South Africa, that Kate and Dick went out to view houses with her cousins. They saw a few houses, and then described to the agent what exactly they were looking for. He took them to a house that was not yet listed or advertised, and as Kate walked into the home, she immediately fell in love with it!

Dick liked it in terms of space but was not convinced on the style. Kate had to convince him that the space was what was important and if he really did not like the colours, they could easily paint it differently! Therefore, they decided to try to get a second viewing alone, as they were distracted on the first day that they had seen it. It was difficult to get the second viewing, as it seemed as though the couple had had a change of heart and did not want to sell anymore. It turned out that they were planning to relocate to Cape Town and were not certain on when the move was going to happen. Eventually, Kate and Dick got around to seeing the place again, and they both agreed that they loved the place. They decided to put in an offer, but, to their disappointment, it was rejected as the owners decided that they did not want to sell anymore.

Kate and Dick continued looking around in the same area to see if they would find something else that they liked. They did see another home that they liked that was in the same price range as the first house they saw. The style however was completely different, and you could not really compare the two houses! Kate and Dick chatted about it and decided to put in a higher offer on the first house as they really liked it! Once again, the offer was rejected.

At the time, Kate was going through her first IV cycle, and Dick did not want to share the disappointing news with her, as he knew how madly in love with the house she was. And so he went to the agent, and he asked the owner how much it would cost to get his wife out of the house as he had previously said she was the one that did not want to let it go. In the end, Kate and Dick paid even more for the house. After a long sixteen months of waiting, Kate and Dick were the proud new owners!

Kate was really taken aback by Dick's kind gesture of going beyond to get her dream house for them!

It was at this point that Dick saw his family's envy over the couple's material success, although he would not admit it. Dick's mother did not congratulate Kate when they got the house besides sending a brief WhatsApp message. Many people, including Dick's uncle, were proud of their achievement. However, Dick's family were green with envy! Eventually, Dick opened up to Kate and said how he yearned for his mom to tell him that she was proud of him, but all she said to him was congratulations!

Even though Kate had not had kids of her own, she could not understand how Dick's own mom could be so jealous of his achievements. After they received the keys for the house, they invited their families over to view the place. The first available weekend, Dick's mother was extremely busy with Dick's sister's wedding preparations and, as a result, they did not come through to see the place. Dick was sad about this.

When Kate learned that Dick's sister was getting married and, by default, she was the one chosen to be the equivalent of a bridesmaid (which in the Hindu tradition is the lady that stands behind the bride on her wedding day), Kate decided it was time to let go of the past and start afresh. The other sister-in-law and older brother were to play the role of her parents.

Kate and Dick went to Thailand for a holiday about four months before his sister's wedding. Kate offered to get the souvenirs for the wedding. The first day that Kate and Dick arrived in Thailand, she wanted to go shopping immediately for the souvenirs. Kate had seen a resin elephant that had a little holder at the top of its head for a tea candle. Dick's sister was pleased and confirmed the number required. It took almost the entire day to sort out as there was no way that Kate and Dick could take these back in their suitcases as the elephants weighed a substantial amount. They had to source a DHL courier to arrange for the shipment. Dick was not impressed with Kate as the first day was wasted, but Kate was pleased to get it out of the way and have the rest of the holiday to relax and enjoy, stress-free!

As Dick's mother stayed in an apartment in a gated complex, space was limited. Kate knew that they would have the house by the time the wedding was to take place. She offered Dick's sister their new home as an alternative venue that could be used to host the traditional rituals in the days leading up to the wedding. Dick did not, in any way, see this as a great gesture, but assumed it was an entitlement, given it was his family! Once his sister decided she did indeed want to take up the offer, she started discussing the arrangements with Dick rather than Kate! Kate found this behaviour strange, as she was the one that originally offered rather than Dick. Kate called her and asked about what she had decided about the offer, and that Dick's sister should let her know what was required from Kate's side.

Kate's sophistication and level of elegance from her wedding lived on eight years later when she was asked by Dick's sister for contact details of the service providers used for various elements in their wedding.

Kate and Dick worked extremely hard to ensure that the minor renovations to their new home were completed on time and all that was in their control was in place to make the wedding a success. Kate's parents were amazing, as always, in fully supporting the couple. Kate could call them at any time during the day and ask them to go and purchase additional supplies for the builders just to ensure that everything was on track and no time was wasted. Although they had already picked out tiles, bathroom fittings etc., there just seemed to never be enough time on a weekend! The builders worked around the clock and even with their meticulous planning, it came down to the very last day!

It is a Hindu tradition that the house is blessed prior to moving into it. Kate and Dick's house prayer was scheduled for the Monday evening. Kate and Dick stayed in the house from the Monday evening. Her dad and mum assisted her during the day to move their kitchenware and the urgent items that were required for the wedding. They decided to move their clothes and the rest of their items after the wedding.

Kate and Dick had three nights in their new home before Kate opened her doors selflessly to Dick's family. They had six family members staying with them, and Dick's mother never bothered to ask Kate if she required any linen, towels or extras to cater for the additional people. Everything was supplied by Kate and Dick. The wedding rituals began on the Thursday evening with the Mehndi evening.

Dick's mother still asked Kate to prepare a pasta dish for the Thursday evening. Kate had taken a day's leave and spent the entire day doing grocery shopping and the last-minute runaround for items that were required. Dick's mother and sister only arrived late that afternoon. The builders were still assisting Kate to assemble the beds in the additional rooms for the guests. Kate still needed to dress the beds with linen, cook, iron their clothes for the evening, shower and be ready! Moreover, if that was not enough, Dick's mother had also asked Kate to grill the chicken in the oven and ensure that was prepared! Thankfully, Dick's aunt arrived, and Kate was so grateful that she could assist her in the kitchen whilst she scrambled to complete her other tasks.

Dick's sister-in-law arrived late as usual. It was routine that Dick's brother and his wife were always late, and now it was acceptable as they used their twins as an excuse for not being punctual! Dick's sister-in-law's contribution for the evening was a salad, which she arrived without! Dick's brother then had to rush off to the shop to purchase this! Of course, this was not a big deal at all for Dick's mother! There were several other things that she offered such as serviettes and candles, but she never delivered. At the last minute, Kate had to go and source these.

When Kate and Dick moved the essentials into the house, the helpers put things into the cupboards haphazardly, and Kate decided she would rather take the time after the wedding to decide where exactly she wanted things to be placed. Kate let Dick's mother always have free reign in their house, as Kate was extremely accommodating and respectful. At the end of the day, she was Dick's mother, and her personality did not allow Kate to challenge her. Dick's mother spent the entire weekend, however, constantly asking Kate where things were and making a fuss over nothing. She seemed extremely anxious and on edge through the various preparations.

Kate's mum was requested to assist with the rituals over the next day, as Dick's mother did not know how to perform them although she was born Tamil. The first cleansing ritual was early in the morning and carried out by all the women. Dick's mother was extremely sad and, once she started crying, she could not stop! All the ladies consoled her and, at the same time, kept telling her not to be upset in front of Dick's sister. This would upset Dick's sister and make her feel guilty for leaving home and her mom. Kate could not understand this at all! Dick's sister was genuinely happy to be getting married, and Dick's mother's behaviour came across as selfish. She was focused on being the victim, thinking about herself and how she was now going to be alone, because her daughter was going to be married and no longer in the house. She also had experienced this herself before, so why would she not be happy that her daughter had found someone that she wanted to marry and spend the rest of her life with?

Bearing this mood in mind, you can imagine what Dick's mother was like over the next few days.

Dick's mother planned the Friday evening ritual. The gentleman that was to set up the marquee arrived with dirty crockery, utensils and did not do a great job with the draping and set-up of the stage where Dick's sister was to sit. The helpers had to wash all the crockery and utensils before laying them out for the guests. Thankfully, Kate's sister had done draping before, and she fixed the draping.

The supplier did not provide a proper light source for the marquee besides the decorative fairy lights. The lighting was most certainly going to be insufficient for the guests. Dick had to rush off and purchase a flood light which had to be positioned in the centre of the marquee to offer adequate lighting. As this was in the middle of winter, which can be cold in Johannesburg, Dick's mother hired heaters; however, these arrived way after the guests arrived. As a result, Dick's mother was in an absolute frenzy and irritable mood. Kate felt that this was unreasonable as everyone chipped in and were going above and beyond to ensure that this wedding would be a great success!

Never had Kate been so happy to sneak in a drink in the scullery with Dick's aunt, just to take the edge off, calm her nerves and prevent her from losing her mind!

The relationship between Dick and his sister was strained at this point. Initially, when the wedding was announced, Kate and Dick were told their roles and Dick's task for the wedding was to be the master of ceremonies. However, about a month before the wedding, Dick was told that he was no longer required to be the master of ceremonies. The bridal couple had chosen a close friend of the groom, and Dick was just to do the toast to the bridal couple.

Kate really felt for Dick the day that he learnt the news; he had literally raised his sister and had been there for her throughout her life. All that Kate could do was acknowledge how selfless he was when it came to his sister, tell him he could be proud of the fatherly role that he played in her life and that he should overlook this choice the bridal couple had made.

The Friday evening celebration ended off with a night of dancing. A song played that night which Kate clearly remembered Dick and his sister dancing to at her 18th birthday. Kate immediately stood up, took Dick by the hand toward his sister and obliged him to dance with her. Kate then went and sat next to her mum and tears filled her eyes as she watched Dick and his sister dance as they did for her eighteenth birthday.

Even during this tough time when Dick was finally seeing the true colours of his family, Kate never manipulated the situation to her advantage. All Kate ever yearned for was for everyone to get along; she wished for a better relationship with Dick's family, between Dick and her family, and between each other's families.

The next morning was the day of the wedding. Dick's sister had done a hair trial at Kate's hair salon but opted to go with someone else that was going to do a house call. However, Dick's mother and her niece had asked Kate to book for their hair styling at her salon. When Kate woke up that morning and got ready, she went to check if Dick's mother and her niece were ready to leave for the hair appointments as she was driving everyone. Dick's sister then informed her that they had cancelled their appointments and were using the hairdresser that she was going to use. Kate could not believe it; Dick's mother did not even bother to tell her that she had changed her plans, even though she had instructed Kate initially to make the appointments.

When Kate returned from the salon, she found Dick's sister in her bedroom. She had decided to use her dressing room and bedroom to get done. Whilst Kate did not mind at all, common courtesy would have been to ask her first as opposed to just take over her only private space. Kate had opened up her entire house, and this was literally her only space.

It was a rollercoaster of a few days, and Kate just wanted to burst out crying. She was exhausted and tired. Kate and Dick had extended themselves selflessly for this wedding. All Kate wanted to do on the day was to go out, get drunk and enjoy the wedding.

Dick's mother sat sobbing throughout the wedding ceremony. The snapshot, if you removed the surrounding scenery, could easily pass for her sitting at a funeral!

Dick delivered his toast which included advice on marriage and relationships. He shared important points to focus on, and Kate was impressed at how his perspective had changed. The one point that stood out was him saying how you needed to put your partner first before anyone else!

Although Dick was not one that enjoyed dancing, Kate and Dick danced the night away and had much fun with his brother and the cousins.

Kate and Dick drove back from the wedding venue with Dick's mother and Kate's parents. Dick's mother did not speak the entire time in the car, and Kate could hear her snivelling. She was still tearful. Dick even had to ask her if she was in the car as a joke!

Kate and Dick dropped her parents off, and Dick and his brother offloaded all the wedding presents at Kate's parents' house. Dick did not want to hold onto the presents until the newlyweds returned from their honeymoon, as there was no secure place at the new house.

The next morning Kate and Dick went to go and fetch the bridal couple from the venue. The last lunch was planned for the family at Kate and Dick's before everyone was to head home. Whilst Kate and Dick were away, an argument occurred between her mum and Dick's mother!

When Kate's parents arrived, Dick's mother immediately asked Kate's mum where were the gifts that were given to Dick's brother and his wife during the ceremony as they stood as parents. Kate's mum said she did not know, and she should ask Dick or his brother as they offloaded the gifts the night before. Dick's mother then claimed that Kate's mum was rude to her, such a bully and spent the entire weekend ruling everything!

When Kate and Dick returned, Kate's mum was upset and came to Dick and Kate to mention what had transpired whilst they were away, and Dick immediately said he was not going to take sides.

They were about to have lunch when the family received a call to say that Dick's uncle (his mother's brother) had passed away. He had been ill in the prior couple of months and had not been at the wedding. Once lunch was done, Dick's mother packed up all her things. The bridal couple were to leave on their honeymoon the following day.

As Dick's mother left the house, Kate was the last person that she said goodbye to. She gave her a false empty hug and said just "thank you" and walked out. She did not acknowledge or appreciate what Kate had done in the months building up to the wedding, and more so in the last few days prior to the wedding.

Dick's mother attended her elder brother's funeral in Durban, and she drove down with her younger brother and his wife and daughter. Dick's younger brother and wife shared with Kate later that the entire way down to Durban, Dick's mother complained about Kate and Kate's parents, and everything negative that occurred during the wedding were as a result of Kate and her parents!

Dick, of course, raised the issue with Kate, and, once he heard his mother's side of the story, he had taken her part. So once again, the recollection of events had been twisted with Dick's mother's perspective. Everything that Kate and her parents had helped with in getting the house ready for the wedding and the preparations for the wedding itself meant nothing at all. Dick could not see beyond his mother's complaints! Kate then agreed to speak to her mum and ask her to please call Dick's mother to apologise for the way she made her feel in order to keep the peace.

It was a big ask of someone. However, Kate knew given the type of person that her mum was, she would do this for her. Kate's mum called Dick's mother in the week to follow. Once she saw the number come up that it was Kate's mum calling, she did not pick up the phone. Kate thanked her mum for trying and told her mum not to bother thereafter.

Kate and Dick then made a decision that they would put this fallout between their mums in the past. It was something that happened between their mums. They were not even present, and they needed to move on and live their lives.

That December, Kate and Dick decided to have a New Year's Eve party/housewarming party as they had not celebrated their new house with the family. When Dick messaged his mother to invite her, she was upset and told him that she could not see herself in the same room as Kate's parents! Dick firmly told her that Kate and he had decided that they would like to have everyone over to celebrate their new home, and that they were all adults and needed to deal with each other! Kate was pleased that he did not fall for her manipulation this time round and gave his mother a realistic perspective.

Dick's sister had her own plans and was just going to drop Dick's mother off. When they arrived, Dick's mother mentioned that she would take a taxi back home once she was ready to go back. Dick completely lost his temper and was very angry with his mother for saying this. An argument broke out between Dick, his sister and Dick's mother. It was cheeky of Dick's mother to say this as Dick always saw to her needs, and he most certainly would not have subjected her to taking a taxi home. He was really upset by her behaviour. Kate did not know what had transpired in the moment, but Dick later shared it with her.

Dick's mother sat in the lounge like a stranger and visitor. Kate's mum even went and offered her snacks and something to drink. It was very awkward, and anyone could easily feel the tension in the room.

Dick refused to call his sister to wish her for New Year's, and he did not want to have anything to do with his mother. It was the first time in eleven years that Dick refused to see his family for his birthday, which followed ten days later.

Dick had not gone out of his way for Kate's previous birthday, and even went as far as telling his uncle that Kate was in a bad space at the time, and he did not know how to please her. As a result, he invited her four closest girlfriends with their partners, and they all had drinks and dinner together at the casino that they were booked into for the night.

This did not phase Kate at all. She went out of her way to make Dick's birthday extra special for him. She chose a rustic hotel just forty-five minutes outside of Johannesburg, which was extremely tranquil, relaxing and situated alongside a stream. They offered an amazing six-course dinner with a wine pairing (the wine pairing part was Kate's treat of course!). Kate also arranged for an archery class as Dick had been speaking about it for a while and was keen to try it out. The following day, Kate booked a half-day spa package at a five-star resort that they had not tried out before. Dick was completely grateful and blown away with all the birthday spoils!

Kate spoke to Dick to convince him that he needed to see his mother and chat about their argument to resolve the disagreement. A few weeks later, it was arranged for him to go and see his mother after work. What do you know, Dick's mother's biggest issue was Kate and her mum during his sister's wedding! She complained that Kate treated her badly, did not compliment his sister, said nasty things about the function and his sister, and that Kate thought that she was better dressed at the reception than his sister was! (Ironically, this is a comment that was made by Dick at the reception, when he whispered to Kate that he thought that his sister's dress was not well chosen, and she looked more elegant!) She went on to say that Kate's mum was an absolute bully, took over her daughter's wedding and was in charge of everything! (Again, completely off the mark since she asked Kate's mum to assist with the rituals as she didn't know what was to be done.) Finally, she claimed that Kate's mum acted as if it was her daughter's wedding. (Again, ironic as she already had the opportunity to experience weddings of two daughters, given that Kate and her sister were already married!)

Dick came home that evening and told Kate that things were resolved with his mother; however, he listed all the issues that were brought up about Kate and her mum. Kate could not believe her ears! It was expected by now that Dick's mother was manipulative and could twist stories, but Kate could not fathom that Dick would believe her and raise them as issues with Kate! She responded to all of Dick's mother's statements to allow him to see her perspective, and eventually she gave up! She explained to Dick what she had offered to his sister and family was selfless, and she had not even shown such kindness to her own sister or parents ever! If Dick nor his family could see her true character and appreciate her generous efforts, she was officially done with Dick's family! This was the highest level of kindness Kate could show to his family! She also mentioned to him that she could no longer visit his family as often as they were, as she knew exactly what they thought of her and was not willing to tolerate or be around such toxic energy.

Kate had never really had any discussions with girlfriends about what goes down in the bedroom. One Saturday afternoon, Kate met two of her girlfriends for drinks, and the conversation came up. The girls openly shared and commented on what they enjoyed with their partners. Kate was extremely embarrassed as she realised that what she always knew deep down inside was now confirmed. She never experienced any of what the girls were talking about with her husband and partner of so many years! Kate was in a relationship with someone for such a long period of time, but could not share or contribute to the conversation. Her intimate interaction with Dick was so restricted and limiting.

As the years evolved and Kate and Dick's relationship grew, it strengthened, and the bond between them continued to develop over time. The couple were never short of challenges when it came to life. Whether it be the adversity of the family dynamics, juggling of their time between their families, Dick prioritising his family over Kate, moving to Bermuda or the final hurdle of the struggle to start a family of their own.

CHAPTER 9
Unconceived

In 2012, in her final year of studying her MBA, Kate decided to convince Dick that it was time that they started to try and plan for a family. Kate had been on the oral contraceptive pill since her second last year in high school and, for this reason, she was under the assumption that it might take a long time to conceive.

Toward the end of July 2012, Kate and Dick had attended a friend's daughter's birthday party. This is when the topic came up again about when the couple were planning to start a family. After that weekend, Kate decided it was time to stop the pill, as she still had until April 2013 to complete and hand in her dissertation. She wanted the pill to work its way out of her system since she had been on it for so many years.

Dick seemed comfortable and open with the idea of starting a family; however, he wanted to control the timing. First, he decided that they would still use an alternative means of contraception until Kate was done with her MBA. Kate, out of desperation, called Dick's mother and asked her to speak to him and explain that the conception would not be immediately, and it was probably going to be a process. Shortly after listening to his mother, Dick then decided to work out which month would be best, based on the star sign that the baby would be potentially born under, and the season in which the birth would take place! He had a preference for a baby born in the summertime rather than the wintertime because of the night feeds! Kate thought that all of this was ridiculous!

As a result, Kate and Dick finally officially started trying to conceive in September of 2012. This was probably the only time that Kate enjoyed the act of sexual intercourse to some degree and, once she had a glass of wine with her dinner, she found it easy for her to relax, get into the mood and get the deed done! Dick would often comment that now that she wanted to have a baby, she seemed to want to have sex more often.

By the end of 2012, nothing had happened besides her awful skin breakouts and intense menstrual cramps. Kate had no need for the use of an ovulation indicator as the pain was so focused and intense, she knew when she was ovulating!

Kate started a new job at the beginning of January 2013, and little did she know the many changes that awaited her.

She decided to find a gynaecologist just in case she did conceive! She managed to secure an appointment almost immediately, despite it being with a specialist in fertility. Kate explained how long she had been on the contraceptive pill and how long they were trying to conceive. The doctor immediately confirmed that something should already have happened. He went on to perform a scan, and he confirmed that Kate had Polycystic Ovarian Syndrome which was causing her Endometriosis.

Polycystic Ovarian Syndrome or PCOS is a condition in which a woman's levels of oestrogen and progesterone are out of balance. This leads to the growth or formation of ovarian cysts (benign masses on the ovaries). PCOS causes irregular menstrual cycles, infertility and excess body weight, facial hair and acne.

Endometriosis is a painful disorder in which the tissue that normally lines the inside of the uterus, known as the endometrium, grows outside the uterus. This misplaced tissue develops into growths and lesions, which respond to the body's monthly menstrual cycle in the same way that the uterine lining does. Each month the tissue builds up, then breaks down and sheds. Normally, menstrual blood flows out of the uterus and out of the body through the vagina but the blood and tissue shed from endometrial growths has no way of leaving the body. This results in internal bleeding, pain, infertility, scar tissue, adhesions and inflammation.

The doctor advised that Kate go in for a laparoscopy, which is a surgery that involves a small incision usually near the belly button and around the pubic line. A tube is inserted through the incisions and carbon dioxide gas is pumped through the tube to inflate the abdomen. Inflating the abdomen allows the surgeon to see the organs more clearly. A laparoscope is then inserted through this tube. The scar tissue or endometriosis is then cut away or removed with a laser beam or electric current (electrocautery).

The doctor was sure that after her laparoscope, Kate and Dick would conceive within three months. The doctor also put her on some medication to balance out the hormones.

Kate was really surprised at the news as she has never been one to be ill or sickly. She was, however, determined to overcome whatever stood in the way of them conceiving and having a child.

The laparoscope was successful, and all the scar tissue and adhesions were successfully removed. Although most of the carbon dioxide is pressed out of the abdomen before stitching up the incisions, some of the gas remains. This can be extremely painful when the bubbles travel upwards and get lodged in the chest area. As a result, severe shoulder pain and discomfort is common. The gas unfortunately cannot be passed but must dissolve in the blood. Kate could not wear any tight clothing or pants for a few weeks. The discomfort is more so in skinny individuals, like Kate.

Three months elapsed, and Kate was still not pregnant. She went back to the doctor, and he advised that the couple needed to do a post coital test. This test examines the interaction between the sperm and mucus of the cervix post coital (after intercourse) and is used in the evaluation of infertility. The test is done one to two days before ovulation when the cervical mucus is thin, allowing the sperm easy movement through the uterus. A sample of the female's cervical mucus is examined under microscope. In Kate's case, there were no sperm seen under the microscope, thus indicating a hostile cervical mucus or environment in the uterus.

The doctor confirmed that Kate was infertile, and the couple would need to try assisted methods for them to conceive. The next option was for them to try artificial insemination.

Artificial insemination is the deliberate introduction of sperm into the uterus to assist with the fertilization when the female is ovulating. The female is required to lie down for about fifteen to forty-five minutes after the insemination to allow the sperm to do their work.

The fertility clinic had a walk-in system for the mornings instead of patients needing to make appointments during the day. Patients would get to the clinic from before six o'clock in the morning to put their names on the list and get into the queue. The doctors would only arrive around seven o'clock and then begin to see patients. There were four doctors and several nurses in the practise; however, the number of patients going through this clinic was phenomenal! On Kate's clinic days, she would have to wake up at 4:30 to make it there on time. She would often nap in the car until the sun was out and she had to go in.

Kate and Dick tried artificial insemination three times with no success. Kate was sad on each occasion that they were not successful, but after each failed attempt she quickly lifted herself up to try again and come back fighting even harder than before.

Kate's mum and dad were away during her artificial insemination procedures, and she saw this as a great time for Dick and her to bond and get closer to each other whilst going through this trying time.

The doctor then suggested IVF. In vitro fertilization is an assisted reproductive technology commonly known as IVF, and is a process whereby the female is given several different medications to stimulate ovulation. A female naturally only produces fifteen to twenty eggs which mature inside the ovaries. Only one to two of the ripest eggs are released into the fallopian tubes.

During the first ten days of the IVF cycle, the female injects several different hormone treatments to control ovulation and egg production.

After the first week, the doctor scans again to check the size of the maturing follicles. Once the follicles have fully developed, another injection is given to prevent premature release of the follicles. Within thirty-four to thirty-six hours later, the mature eggs are collected by needle aspiration whilst under sedation.

The freshly collected sperm is then placed with the eggs in a glass petri dish and incubated at a specific temperature, in certain environmental conditions and with infection control for about four days. About two to five days after fertilization has taken place, the most viable embryos (fertilized eggs) are selected. One to three embryos can be placed in the uterus, and it's up to the couple to decide on the number. The embryos are placed into the uterus using a catheter (thin flexible plastic tubing) that is inserted through the cervix. The remaining viable embryos can then be frozen for future transfers and attempts.

Unfortunately, the outlay of cash required for IVF treatment is significant and is not covered by any South African medical insurance. Although Dick wasn't totally convinced, after they discussed affordability, they started with their first IVF in September 2013.

Everyone knew about the laparoscope and Kate's initial diagnosis. She personally decided not to share the artificial insemination and IVF with any friends or family that she felt were not supportive of them as a couple. She would share with those who were more supportive of her as the main individual going through all the medical procedures and treatments. The only family that knew about her subsequent treatments were her parents and Dick's uncle that lived in Pietermaritzburg. Kate also shared it with close girlfriends of hers that were very supportive.

Dick would constantly fight with Kate about not sharing it with his mum, brother and sister. Kate had to keep stating her case and emphasised that his family did not show any support, instead his mum and family would often comment about how Kate's flawless skin had changed and how she had so many vry puisies, which translated into English means pimples because of making out with your partner. Kate felt the comments and behaviour were inappropriate as she was over thirty years old at that stage. They were all aware of the diagnosis and her hormone imbalance preventing her from becoming pregnant, and overlooked how desperate the couple were to get pregnant.

Kate decided that she would place too much pressure on herself if she had to inject herself. Therefore, she would arrange the vials, have everything ready and would ask Dick to please inject them.

They were many early mornings at the clinic, lots of needles, injections, bloods and procedures. However, she was determined that she was going to get this right and be successful. Dick really loved kids, and she felt guilty that she could not make this possible for them. He had a difficult past, and she felt guilty that he had to go through this with her. Kate would often ask him how he felt, and he would say that it did not really affect or bother him.

During their initial insemination rounds, Kate had a very strong feeling that she may have a slightly overactive immune system. As mentioned before, she never really got sick ever. An autoimmune disease can, of course, have a detrimental effect on a foetus, and so she asked the doctor to run bloods on this to confirm.

It was confirmed that her results were borderline and not in the confirmed elevated range; however, she still asked to be treated as though they were elevated, just to make sure they were covered in this regard. This entailed having an additional weekly injection given intramuscularly by the nurse after the embryo transfer.

Kate went through the stimulation process and was incredibly grateful that she did not experience any of the horrible side effects from all the high doses of hormones. She felt bloated, but understandably so given that she had so many follicles growing at a proliferated rate inside of her! She had to also drink at least two litres of water a day at a minimum!

Kate ended up with six fertilized embryos. Kate and Dick decided to transfer two embryos the first round. When the embryologist and doctors look at the embryos under the microscope, there is no guarantee that they will attach to the uterus once transferred. Any slight or ever so small genetic mutation is picked up on and immediately rejected by the body.

After the transfer is done, several medications continue to be taken as the body is deceived into believing that it is pregnant. There are also other immune suppressants that are taken to prevent the body from rejecting the embryo. Then, it's just a waiting game for a further one to two weeks before bloods are done to check for the positive or negative result.

On the Sunday before Kate was due to go in for her bloods, her stomach already started cramping and she knew there was a big possibility that this meant it did not work again! She still went in on the Monday morning with every bit of fighting energy and hope. After her bloods were taken and she was waiting for the nurse and doctor to discuss them with her, she needed to go to the toilet. As Kate had suspected, she had already started menstruating. A few minutes later, it was confirmed by the doctor that the transfer did not take, and she was not pregnant. Kate was extremely sad, frustrated and hurt. Why was this happening to her?

She had a good cry and called her mum when she got to the car to tell her that it did not work again. Dick immediately suggested taking a break before going into the next cycle.

It did not take Kate very long to bounce back with fighting spirit and be ready to try again, but as suggested by Dick, she took a break. The remaining four embryos were, in the meantime, frozen.

She saw her doctor in-between, and he suspected that perhaps the endometriosis had returned as it was more than a year since her last laparoscope. During each cycle, her lining would not thicken to the right diameter no matter how much of medication she took.

They had an extremely long break in between as they bought a new house, completed renovations and then hosted Dick's sister's pre-wedding rituals at the house. It was a most stressful time, and she certainly could not have also attempted a round of fertility.

Kate also decided to give homeopathy a chance and consulted with a homoeopathist who specialised in radionics. Radionics is an alternative medicine that uses a radionic instrument to identify, analyse and treat any imbalances in a patient's energy or unique energy patterns of disease. She ended up with thirty-six different containers of little white tablets that need to be dissolved under the tongue! Moreover, they had to be dissolved in that specific order! She looked a bit crazy or very ill, sitting at her desk at work with all these containers on her desk and popping pills. She honestly was willing to try anything!

In September 2014 after her break, Kate decided to re-do the laparoscope and then do a transfer thereafter.

Life around her continued, and no one at work except for close friends knew what she was going through. People would offer advice about relaxing, but it was exceedingly difficult to identify with any of them, except for those friends that had similar fertility challenges and experiences. It was a physically, emotionally and mentally draining process to go through. No money in the world could guarantee that you would be successful at it either. It was a gamble each month with a more than seventy percent chance that she would be unsuccessful!

Kate had a friend that conceived both her kids naturally directly after a laparoscope. She was subjected to attending baby shower after baby shower. She witnessed all her friends around her fall pregnant and had to smile and say to herself her time would come. Her biological clock was ticking, and the next step in their marriage was to have a child. People would comment and ask, "so when are you starting a family?" and it was difficult to keep composed and answer when the time is right it would happen for them. Dick tried to understand what Kate was going through, but from his behaviour, comments and actions at times she really did not believe he understood or fully supported her.

Kate was forever grateful for her mum, who was always there to support her, and even to accompany her to appointments if Dick's schedule did not allow for him to be present.

Kate's second laparoscope went well, and they tried a frozen transfer of two embryos thereafter. The embryos are defrosted and monitored for viability before transfer. Once again, she was on a regime of several drugs. This time, her mum was with her for her final blood results of the process. Again, they waited for the doctor and nurse to share the results. It was like sitting and waiting to hear if you have passed or failed an exam. Kate wanted nothing more than to be pregnant. Kate and Dick's relationship was ready for them to have a baby. And the result was a negative! A wave of emotions flooded over her as she broke down with her mum. She felt anger, hurt, frustration and disappointment. She called Dick and shared the news with him. He was sorry about the news and felt she should really take a break, and it would happen naturally. How on earth was it going to happen naturally when she had a medical condition that was preventing this from happening?!

Kate's hair was brittle and not in a healthy condition. She had to stop highlighting her hair because of the impact of the hormones on her hair. She really felt awful about the way she looked. She indeed had flawless skin before trying to fall pregnant, and now looked like a teenager again with full-blown acne and scarring. Her confidence was exceptionally low as she gave selflessly to attempt to fall pregnant for Dick and her.

A message from within her kept coming up ... *You need to put yourself first! You cannot keep doing this.* Kate felt drained and tired. As per Dick's convincing, the couple decided to take another break.

They decided in the meantime to focus their attention on choosing the dogs that they both always wanted. Dick had done the research, and he found a breeder for a Labrador which was the type of dog that he always wanted. Kate was not keen on large breed dogs, but they each got to choose their own.

Kate met Titus on the 15th February 2015, and he immediately connected with her and stole her heart! They visited him at the breeder until he was eight weeks old and could finally come home in March of that year. Titus filled the emptiness inside of Kate, and the inability to conceive. Titus loved her unconditionally; he filled their new home with a new energy, he made it complete!

Maria is the woman that took care of the house and stayed on the property. After a few months of working for Kate and Dick, she met someone and very occasionally went to her friends and to see her new boyfriend over the weekends. She probably met this new boyfriend twice.

One weekend when Kate and Dick had to go to his family, and Kate noticed that Maria seemed very uncomfortable and in pain. She asked her what was wrong, and Maria explained that she had got her period and had severe cramps. Kate gave her some pain tablets and then they left.

Kate sent Maria a message later in the afternoon to see how she was doing. Maria said she had been vomiting and was really feeling ill. She asked Kate to get her some medication. On Monday morning, she said she felt a bit better. Later that afternoon before Kate got home from work, Maria sent her a message to say that she was in extreme pain. Kate rushed home and took her to the doctor.

When they arrived at the doctor, they ran a urine test and the routine vitals. Kate was still completing the paperwork whilst the nurse took Maria in and started with her vitals. As Kate entered the room, she overheard the nurse saying, "it is positive, but wait for the doctor to talk to you". Kate was in complete shock, could this be real, Maria was pregnant! Kate had to keep calm and composed. Once the nurse left the room, Maria told her it was not possible because she had not skipped any of her periods, and she was convinced she was not pregnant.

They waited for the doctor to come and talk to them. The doctor suspected an ectopic pregnancy but needed Kate to take Maria for an ultrasound to the hospital to confirm the diagnosis.

An ectopic pregnancy is one in which the fertilized egg implants somewhere other than the uterus, typically in the fallopian tube. When an ectopic pregnancy ruptures, bleeding can be severe and even life-threatening.

By this time, it was already after hours. Kate and Maria then made their way to the nearest hospital to try and get the ultrasound done to understand the next steps.

With the referral letter in hand, Kate attempted to find out if the radiologist was still in and if Maria could be seen. The radiologist was closed, but they were then told to sign in as an outpatient. After filling a completely new set of forms, they finally saw a doctor only for him to say that they needed to return the following day as no one could assist them at that time.

Kate was tired, hungry, emotionally drained and extremely frustrated at the poor service and the incorrect information that was shared! They finally decided to go home and wake up early the next morning to go in to do the ultrasound. Kate had messaged Dick through the afternoon and kept him posted.

Once she got home and Maria went to her room, Kate finally had her own space to process what she had just learnt. She could not believe how unfair life seemed. Maria had visited her boyfriend just twice in six months, was supposedly using protection, did not want to have any more kids (she already had two) and fell pregnant! By no means was she not empathetic toward Maria, but she could not suppress the emotions and pain that surfaced. She had faced a struggle for over two and a half years trying to conceive, and now, due to negligence on Maria's part, she fell pregnant, just like that!

Kate had something to eat, and Dick was watching TV as she finally broke down. He immediately asked her why she was upset and said that she should not be making this about her, rather it was about Maria! Kate initially tried to explain to him from her perspective that she was the one throughout the afternoon that had to be strong and supportive of Maria and her situation. This was now her space and time to go through her emotions and deal with the pain of so desperately wanting to fall pregnant, whilst Maria fell pregnant so easily. Yes, it ended up not being a normal pregnancy or full-term pregnancy, but she still conceived very easily. Kate eventually gave up on explaining why she was crying or how she felt. She went to the room, took a shower and went to sleep.

The next morning, Kate had to wake up early and take Maria to the hospital. On their way in the car, Maria said to her "Ma'am, I wish this was happening to you ". Maria's emotional intelligence was much higher than Dick's for sure! She understood what Kate was feeling and whilst going through this with her and was considerate of Kate's own personal struggle to conceive. She did not know what to say to Maria, but Kate had to really swallow hard and fight the tears from falling. She wanted to be strong for her again.

Kate proceeded to have the crucial conversation with Maria about contraception and taking responsibility for herself, especially since she was the one who did not want any more kids. It turned out her boyfriend did not use a condom, and Maria was under the impression he did.

Kate and Maria arrived at the hospital where the ultrasound was done. She went in with Maria and tried to listen to understand what was happening. The assistants would not give her the results and said the doctor would phone the referring doctor. When they called the referring doctor, she was unavailable, and never called back with the results or next steps!

They were given the scans and a report, and so Kate decided to open the report. It was indeed confirmed as a ruptured ectopic pregnancy. It was critical that Maria got medical surgery immediately.

Maria was not on Kate or Dick's medical insurance, and they could by no means pay for her to go to a private hospital. Kate had to send her to a government hospital the following day. The doctor that saw Maria was an absolute blessing! She was taken in immediately, and the surgery was performed due to the seriousness. The surgery was successful, and Kate and her mum went to visit Maria before she was discharged.

All through this, Dick did not understand how tough it was on Kate, and how she put aside her own feelings and emotions to be supportive of Maria. It was only when Kate was alone that she could reflect and deal with her feelings.

Maria was very humbled by the experience, and Kate was grateful that she was able to seek good medical help and that she survived this life-threatening experience.

A few months elapsed, and Kate decided it was time to try a new intervention. She had now been with the same fertility clinic and had tried different treatment options in a stepwise approach to no avail. Whilst she believed most treatment regimens would have a commonality between them, she decided to go to the other big fertility clinic in Johannesburg.

A friend of Kate's recommended the doctor, and she managed to get an appointment within two weeks. Dick attended the first appointment with Kate. She was amazed at how much time the doctor took to look at her medical file and history. At her previous clinic, it felt like a train station, and everyone seemed to be on the same treatment protocol just with slight variances. The doctor did not agree with certain medication that Kate was on for the PCOS, as he only agreed with endometriosis as a diagnosis. This doctor had a confident plan on how to do things differently to ensure success.

Kate was thrilled! Finally, they were going to conceive! All that they needed to do was check their finances to ensure that they had the outlay of cash that was required, and they were good to go!

The following day, Kate and Dick discussed the new strategy and plan. She had received a quote from the doctor, and they had an estimate on the costing. They were going to start a new cycle of IVF but via a different method, namely intra-cytoplasmic sperm injection (ICSI), which involves the injection of a single sperm directly into an egg instead of fertilization taking place in a petri dish where many sperm are placed in close proximity to the egg. This method was, of course, more expensive than the normal IVF cycle.

Kate and Dick were extremely good at saving money each month. They had enough money in their savings to cover this treatment, but Dick was not comfortable using all their savings, as this would mean that they would not have any spare cash around should they need it. Kate was extremely upset when

Dick explained this to her, as he did not mention this prior to sourcing the new clinic. She was in high spirit after the break and wanted to start again and go full speed at getting this right. At the same time though, given how stressful the IVF process is, Kate did not want to go into it without Dick being fully on board. If he said they didn't have the money for it, then she had to let it go. Dick reassured Kate that they would wait for his bonus the following year and then start with the new cycle.

CHAPTER 10
Losing Her Identity

When Kate met Dick, she was a girl that was extreme-ly naïve and had not been exposed to the real world. Many people might describe her as being "mollycoddled". She completed school and chose to attend a local university. Kate stayed with her parents and was extremely fortunate to have everything provided.

In her first year of studying, her mum would drop her off at the university. This continued until she got her driving license and a car, and was later able to drive herself to the university. All meals were taken care of, and she could order her favourites and have snacks delivered to the study during the long hours she put in studying. Her laundry was done, and she had no worries in the world besides to study her hardest, do her best and complete her degree.

Perhaps she was never faced with many situations in which she needed to voice her opinion or speak up? She was thus a very reserved and introverted individual. Her initial dif-ficulties with Dick therefore proved to be challenging. Kate was brought up in a household in which they would never go to bed upset with each other and there were very few disagreements or arguments. Whilst this might sound strange, it was really a case of a family that operated in unison. Kate got along well with her parents, and they rarely encountered any differences.

Dick met all the criteria Kate imagined in a potential partner, and she therefore openly trusted the process. Whilst Dick's firm and inflexible character often scared her, she felt that her inexperience in the world allowed his opinions and thoughts to take preference over hers. In general, Kate was a very accommodating person, whether it be with friends or family. She would easily be able to set aside her choices for someone else's preference.

Kate spent many hours in the company of Dick's family. Whilst initially she was very shy, young and naïve, it did not take her very long to realise the agenda of his family. Dick was the pillar of strength both emotionally and financially, and nothing was going to come between them and Dick. However, Kate did not believe that they were very supportive of Dick when they were struggling in their marriage, dealing with the fertility challenges or just celebrating their achievements. It was almost as though they would most probably have preferred to see Kate and Dick apart than together. Dick played the father figure in his family. This role was translated into Kate's and Dick's marriage, and, although Kate was a responsible, educated and well-rounded individual, Dick defaulted to a father figure once again, rather than her husband or equal. He would often speak down to Kate in an authoritarian tone, and he always knew the best solution or choice in any given situation. Kate allowed Dick to treat her this way, and it was not until the last three years of their relationship that she began to stand up for herself and speak up if she disagreed.

Kate's intention was never to have Dick to herself, but rather to be accepted by his family and feel a part of their family. She wanted to be respected as Dick's wife, the woman he had chosen to spend his life with, the woman that cared for him more than she did herself, the woman that loved Dick no matter what and the woman that more than fulfilled her duties as a wife. Kate never felt she was integrated fully or made to feel welcomed by Dick's family. She never felt comfortable spending time with Dick's family and would often remain reserved. After the initial greeting and scanning of her body from head to toe with their gaze, and check in on how the week was, there was no further conversation that took place. Everyone sat around the TV, ate and chatted. Kate rarely felt comfortable to just openly talk or engage in conversation with them, which was challenging for Kate as she was a very sociable person that made friends and meaningful connections easily.

Kate dreaded the weekends, as this meant many hours with Dick's family and feelings of loneliness, discomfort and self-judgment. Her self-confidence was extremely battered. Kate always felt in competition with Dick's family. Perhaps Dick's sister looked up to her and desired to emulate her in a way, and this might have been the reason for her behaviour. However, Kate just wanted to be given credit for who she was, her uniqueness and love that she presented.

Kate yearned to be accepted, appreciated and valued by Dick's family. She did not envisage this to be such a trying task given that many friends and family saw her for who she truly was and what she had to offer. Kate was making way too many sacrifices way too often. She was adapting who she was and getting no reciprocation or appreciation for all the effort she continued to put in daily.

Kate was extremely grateful when Dick's twin nieces were born, as this was a distraction and change of focus within his family. She often directed her attention and energy toward them instead, and enjoyed spending time playing and doing activities with them!

As the years went on and Kate grew in maturity, she could not wrap her head around the concept of her lack of confidence around Dick's family. This was contrasting to her working environment, in which she was highly confident in all aspects of her work and in her ability to deliver her opinion so an informed decision to be made. There were times that Dick's family would even discuss medical topics and not openly ask Kate for her input, even though this was her field of work. She tried so hard to put all of this aside; however, it most definitely affected her in a negative way. Kate could not share this with Dick or her family and often felt very alone.

At the same time, Kate was of the belief that this was her path in life, and she had to live it. She did not believe that she had a choice. Kate was taught that you persist and persevere until you succeed.

Dick would have made an excellent lawyer! He had the ability to argue any point, and could often win over a person and get them to agree with his opinion.

Dick was very strong-minded, and Kate struggled with this for the greater part of their relationship. She was extremely afraid of him initially when it came to conflict, or if they had differing opinions on a topic. Kate most certainly was never honest with him as far as how she felt about his family, as he would always get extremely defensive.

When Kate first met Dick, he had told her that he did not drink any alcohol because he disliked the taste. Furthermore, his dad was an alcoholic, and his brother had been tested for the gene, which was confirmed. Although Dick was not tested, he felt very strongly when it came to the subject of alcohol. He did not want Kate to drink any alcohol ,and went as far as saying that if she did, she would have to brush her teeth first before kissing him!

Kate, on the other hand, grew up in an environment in which her parents allowed her and her sister to enjoy alcohol in their presence. The family would drink socially especially during family get-togethers. Dick's request was rather strange, but nonetheless, Kate obliged and gave up drinking alcohol! Dick was firm in his beliefs and ways of thinking.

Whilst Dick was extremely tough on Kate, he was extremely accommodating toward his mother and sister. Dick's mother would easily convince him of her opinion, and often played on his emotions and used her status of being a single parent and the victim to gain his favour. Dick was extremely loyal and a pillar of strength to his family, and Kate knew upfront that he supported them financially. This continued throughout their relationship until the mortgage on his mother's house was paid off when she retired from teaching.

Although Kate and Dick's backgrounds differed, and Kate's parents were financially secure, Dick did not allow her to just spoil her family or her parents. She would be required to explain why she needed to buy them a gift. Kate always felt guilty because her parents were always there for her. Even after marriage, they would run any errands for her and Dick that they could not get to on a Saturday morning. Kate's mum would cook for them, and she would not force them to have the meal at her home, but would let them take the food away to allow them free time alone. Kate could ask her parents to help with absolutely anything, and they would be there without a complaint and happy to assist!

The monetary value that was spent on each other's siblings and parents for birthdays and celebrations were identical. Dick financially contributed to the running of his mother's home every month. Dick's sister sat at home for a period in which she only had one subject to complete to receive her bachelor's degree. During this time, she never attempted to get a part-time job to assist her mom or to start saving for her honours degree, which she wished to do the year after. As a result, Kate and Dick ended up paying for her honours year. When Dick's brother was in financial difficulty, Dick loaned him money and gave him his car for free to use in the running of his personal business. Dick always wanted to help and assist others in a generous way. However, Kate had to accept that Dick was never going to be fair when it came to how differently their families were treated, be it quality time spent or the amount of financial assistance offered.

All Kate ever craved was the ability to show her parents that she appreciated them by spoiling them occasionally, whether this be a surprise bunch of flowers for her mum or taking them out for a meal. Dick's mother always got first preference when it came to Mother's Day, Diwali (which is the Indian Festival of Lights), Christmas or New Year's Day. Kate and Dick had to always visit Dick's family first, and then they would go to Kate's family later in the evening. The reason given was that Dick's mother needed to go to bed early. She would then also feed them so much of food that they would not be able to eat much when they got to Kate's family! Kate and Dick always had to invite his family over for a braai (what the rest of the world would call a barbeque) to their place, but they would not do the same for Kate's family unless she raised the issue.

Dick was extremely strict with Kate when it came to finances. Kate would refer to him as the Minister of Finance in their household! They had their own separate bank accounts; however, Dick had access to Kate's account and full insight into everything that she spent. He had an Excel spreadsheet of all their income and expenses. At the end of the month, he would reconcile the spreadsheet with the bank statements considering every rand and cent. They each had an allowance which they could spend on anything. Kate asked permission for her allowance to roll over if not used, and the option to take an early advancement on it if she saw something that she really liked and wanted to purchase! Whilst this allowed them to save a lot, Kate often felt like Dick treated her even worse than her dad when it came to controlling her finances! She really was not careless with money and was not like the stereotypical woman who would go out on binge shopping sprees or who lived beyond her means. Prior to marrying Dick, she had her own credit card and did not go wild at all! Instead, she saved each month's salary prior to their wedding. She would have thought that this would have demonstrated her ability to take care with money, but this unfortunately was not the case!

There were often occasions in which things were charged against her allowance; however, Dick could get an item paid for from their joint pool of cash. The one that stood out was when she decided to study her MBA. As their apartment was small, Kate needed to sit at the dining room table to study. They had an open loft area above the dining room which was the TV room. Dick was big into gaming and enjoyed playing video games with a lot of violence and shooting. As a result, he went and purchased a set of the top-line cordless headphones so that he would not disturb Kate whilst she was studying. The headphones were not counted against Dick's allowance. At the same time, Kate chose to purchase a laptop bag to carry her laptop and textbooks when meeting friends to study and discuss assignments. Dick, however, deducted the money for the laptop bag from Kate's allowance! He struggled to understand Kate's perspective. She spent some time convincing him how unfair it was!

As Kate began her MBA, Dick also warned her that she should not ask him for any help. He had managed to complete his studies part-time, on his own, so he was not prepared to help her. He said that this was a decision she had made, and she needed to get on with it on her own. Kate found this quite harsh, as Dick had a lot of work experience, and she thought that she would be able to bounce ideas off him and perhaps be able to discuss case studies with him. In the end, Kate insisted he help her with her data analysis for her dissertation as this was his day job! It was hurtful as Dick's sister would go around to their place for Dick to assist her with her studies and work. His sister followed in his footsteps and studied the same degree as him. He was, of course, more than willing to assist her. Kate could not help but feel that she was unfairly treated by Dick.

Dick was always in charge of most things, and this included the brightness of the lights as they ate their dinner in front of the TV. It drove Kate mad that she could not see what she was eating on most occasions and had to argue for the dimmer switch to be turned on brighter!

Kate was never a person that was into fitness or physical training. She started physical training when she met Dick, but always struggled to get into the routine of it and to maintain it. The gym contract that was taken out was through their medical insurance and required that one attended gym at least twice a month for the year. Kate disliked the gym so much that she would just go past to swipe her tag, and not go into the actual gym to train.

Eventually, due to them travelling, Kate miscalculated the number of times that she had swiped her gym tag. Her gym membership was revoked, and she was penalised. She was also punished by Dick! She then decided in 2015 that with all the stress of trying to fall pregnant, it made sense to exercise. She got a mobile personal trainer to come train her at home. The rates were more expensive; however, Dick had a fully kitted out gym that was set-up at their new home. Dick had spent a fortune creating the gym room. It was impressive, with rubber gym floor mats, mirrors from ceiling to floor, a full range of dumbbells, and all your basic equipment. The cost of Kate's personal trainer, however, had to come out of her allowance as she had irresponsibly revoked her gym contract!

Due to Kate and Dick's differing personalities, they could never agree on watching a movie at the cinema. Initially, Kate had chosen most of the movies they watched, but as the relationship went on, Dick almost always chose the movie that they watched. Dick believed that it was not necessary to watch romantic comedies or any other genre except science fiction on the big screen, as this was required for the sound and special effects.

Dick loved watching TV. It was routine for him to go home, greet Kate, change out of his work clothes and retire immediately to the TV room until dinner was served. If Kate required assistance with anything, he would do it and go back to the TV immediately. Kate had always envisaged her husband sitting with her in the kitchen whilst she prepared the meal. She enjoyed chatting and connecting with people and had thought this would be a great time to catch up on each other's day. Once dinner was ready, Kate and Dick would eat in front of the TV, and Kate would not dare say anything to interrupt Dick's programme. He would get upset with her, because he would need to pause it! They could never just sit in the house and connect with each other and have a conversation, the TV always had to be on, or they had to be watching a movie.

Dick enjoyed routine and structure, and Kate was in some ways the same when it came to her work. However, she did enjoy spontaneity in her personal life, and the unique experiences that life has to offer. Dick always preferred things being planned way in advance and was not very flexible when it came to Kate wanting to be spontaneous. Kate would often just want to get into his convertible, go for a drive out into the countryside, have a lovely meal and enjoy the surroundings.

Whilst Dick was extremely romantic earlier on in their relationship and went through a lot of effort to think of the smaller details to make Kate feel special and appreciated, this quickly dissipated after getting married. Gifts for special occasions became a defined monetary value, and Kate and Dick would go out and purchase their own gifts. Kate felt it to be impersonal as opposed to any thought and intent behind the choice of a gift for a loved one. The one thing that Dick continued to do well from the beginning of their relationship was to write or type her a message on their anniversary and on her birthday instead of buying a card from the shop. Kate treasured these letters and always looked forward to reading what Dick had written. It was an affirmation and insight into how he truly felt about her. He also had a particularly good way with words! This is the anniversary wish that Dick wrote to Kate on their 9th wedding anniversary:

"Happy 9th Anniversary my Angel!!!
For this Anniversary I would like to tell you 9 reasons why I
love you so much!
Your amazing determination to overcome
all odds and obstacles
Your beautiful soft heart filled with compassion and love
Your dedication to me and our relationship
(which is crystal clear)
Your sense of style and class that is unique to you
Your delicious cooking (which you do in no time)
Your spirit and soul which is so illuminatingly beautiful
Your nurturing nature which is caring and kind
Your ability to attract the best people into your life
Your love for me
I am so proud to call you my wife.
You make me a better man just by being with me.
Having you in my life means that I'm a good person.
It means that I have been blessed with the best and that I
can truly be grateful for what I have received in life.
You are the best partner I could hope for
to journey through life with.
I love you more and more each day!
You are my Angel!
Thank you for 9 amazing years that keep getting better!
Mucho Gracias Seniorita a.k.a Titus' mommy! ;)"

Dick was very fussy when it came to Kate's choice in clothes, dress sense, length of her hair, whether she wore make-up or not and whether her nails were painted or not. Whilst he always wanted the girl next door type of look which was effortless for Kate because of her love for jeans and casual nature, he still had a strong opinion when it came to what shoes or clothes she chose to wear! He hated platform heels and, therefore, Kate never owned a pair! He preferred longer length hair and if ever Kate got it cut too short, he would make it known that he was not happy! Kate did, however, manage to get away with straightening her hair, as this was how it had been when he had met her. Although he preferred her hair in its naturally curly state, she would always straighten it. Kate only left her hair curly when they were on holiday in a humid climate when straightening was aimless! Dick hated make-up and whilst Kate agreed with him that a natural look was always the most beautiful, she did wear foundation and base whilst going through her fertility treatments as her skin had a lot of scarring, and she was ashamed to go out without it being hidden.

Dick always got his way with Kate, and her lack of confidence and depleted self-love always resulted in her giving in and allowing Dick to dominate and control her. She would selflessly allow Dick his preferences over hers. She went more than the extra mile to win over his family's approval, which to her disappointment, never materialised.

CHAPTER 11
Her Greatest Gift Received

It was an ordinary Tuesday afternoon after work. Kate called Dick whilst she was out running errands at the shopping mall to confirm the specifications of the decoder that they needed to purchase for Maria's room. Kate also asked Dick what he fancied eating for dinner so that she could grab the required ingredients before making her way home. He said it was okay, they could just make instant noodles for dinner; she did not need to cook anything.

Kate arrived home and found Dick in the kitchen preparing the noodles. Not long after he had greeted her, he said he needed to speak to her after they were done eating. Kate was uneasy with where this was coming from and what it meant. It was close to 12 years at this stage that she had known Dick. Throughout their relationship, Dick seldom initiated instances to sit down and discuss a particular matter that may have been bothering either of them. Kate's mind started to race with numerous potential scenarios in anticipation of what the news could potentially be. She had about three possible scenarios quickly drawn out in her head.

Her first guess was that he wanted to address the now strained relationship between his family, and herself in particular, with his mother. Kate expected at some stage that he would eventually pressure her again and say that she had to see his family routinely and could not avoid them. Her second and third guess were similar in that either his sister or-sister-in-law was pregnant, and he knew that the news would be challenging for her.

Kate could not eat her noodles as she just wanted to hear what the conversation was going to be about. She eventually got halfway through and decided to ask Dick to start talking.

He started off by saying that every year since they were married, he would in some way bring up the topic that he felt that their relationship lacked chemistry and good intimacy. A few years ago, he decided to give up on this aspect and what it meant to him since all the other boxes were ticked in terms of what he wanted in a wife or partner. However, he now realised that he could not go on living his life giving up this passion. By passion, he did not just mean the physical act of sex, but rather the connection. He felt he had 80% of everything that he had ever imagined in a partner with Kate, but the lack of chemistry was integral to who he was as an individual. As a result, he wanted a divorce.

Kate was astounded, not at his description of the lack of chemistry between them, but what hit home very hard was that Dick wanted a divorce, and she was not part of his decision. He had made his mind up and was merely informing her. A host of emotions flooded in. She felt a pit in her stomach, her hands and feet were clammy, her heart was racing, and, at times, she felt as if a sharp knife was cutting through it; her breath was short, and her head hurt and wanted to explode.

Dick tried to console Kate, and apologised for all the pain that was to come her way, and for the fact that he was giving up on them and all that they had built together over the years. However, he was very sure of his choice.

Although Kate was angry, her first reaction was to fight for their relationship. She questioned his decision, and asked how come he persisted for so long if he was supposedly miserable and had been sacrificing who he truly was.

Many questions ran through her mind. Why on earth did he want to start a family with her – just two weeks prior, they had visited the new fertility specialist! How could this be possible if this is what he really had on his mind? Why did he arrange for their new puppy Leah to be flown to them from a breeder in Cape Town just six days before this? There were many long-term life decisions that were made in a normal way, and Kate definitely did not see this one coming. Less than two months prior, Kate had also changed her car, as they needed a large enough vehicle to transport Titus and the new puppy that was later to arrive. It was no wonder she had missed the signs!

Kate was angered that Dick was merely telling her what he wanted and there was no room for any discussion. It was not a case of him sitting her down, sharing his feelings and thoughts, and asking how she felt and what she thought.

Kate and Dick had been through a great deal as a couple, and she truly believed that they could overcome anything that came their way. She believed that their relationship had stood the test of time from the challenges, like family, relocating overseas and the fertility struggle. She really believed that they were at the pinnacle of their marriage.

Kate could not convince Dick otherwise, and her efforts at this stage were futile. Emotions were high, she was still in extreme shock at the news, so decided to go out for a breather. She needed to fill petrol in her car. She had to drive out the following day to a work conference and was not going to have enough time in the morning. Dick could see that Kate was still really upset. He said he thought she was going out to do something stupid to hurt herself, but he didn't make any attempts to stop her.

Kate went to the petrol station and called a girlfriend. She immediately agreed to meet Kate at a restaurant close by. Dick kept sending Kate messages saying he knew she needed time to think things through, but he needed to know that she was safe and that he still cared and loved her.

When Kate met her friend, she was still of the same mindset that she could solve this. She knew it was just a bump in their path, and she would be able to return home and convince Dick that they could work through this all. That is what they did – made things work no matter how difficult the circumstances. Kate's friend was supportive and listened to Kate's thoughts and feelings. After a few hours of chatting, she left, knowing that her friend was happy to support her in whatever choice she was going to make.

Kate returned home and got ready for bed. She did not put on any lights and could not bear to glance to Dick's side of the bed.

Kate could not fall asleep; she was tossing and turning in bed and her mind was active and constantly replaying over the last few hours. She eventually turned around to Dick's side of the bed only to realise that he was not in the bed! This made Kate even angrier! Dick had made the decision that they should divorce and moved out all in the same evening?!

Kate jumped out of the bed and stormed into the next room only to find Dick fast asleep. She started yelling and asking how come he was not sleeping in their bed, and he said it felt right that after he asked for the divorce to move out into another room. Again, Kate tried to reason with him. Then reality sunk in, it was done for real, their marriage was over.

Kate got very little sleep that night, if any. She was extremely tired the next morning and when her alarm went off and her eyes opened, the first thought that came to mind was the harsh reality. It was real; Dick had asked her for a divorce, she was going to be divorced.

Both puppies slept in Kate and Dick's bedroom in their secure crates at night. The breeder had advised them to get these. The crates kept them out of mischief and, at the same time, made them feel protected and secure. Dick would always wake up before Kate and would open them for the puppies to go out first to relieve themselves. The first morning after Dick had moved out into the next bedroom, Titus was immediately thrown off routine. When Kate opened his crate, he immediately ran to Dick's side of the bed. It really broke Kate's heart to watch him. Leah was still settling in. It was only six nights that she had been with them.

As Kate got ready for work, Dick came into their bedroom and said there was something he needed to share with her. Her immediate thought was *what now?! Can this get any worse?*

Dick proceeded to tell her that he had contacted a friend of theirs the previous day and asked for a referral to a medium.

A medium is a person who traditionally speaks in one way or another to the dead. A medium obtains messages from the spirit world in different ways. Some may receive intuitive information, by means of images and words, which appear as mental impressions that are then passed onto the living person attending the reading.

Dick had attended a reading the previous afternoon, just hours before he asked Kate for the divorce. Dick's dad had passed on more than four years prior, and he had never made peace with his father nor forgave him for the negative interactions that he had with him.

Dick shared that during the reading, his dad had come through in spirit and asked permission to speak to Dick. Dick had enquired about why he had behaved the way he did and done all the things that he did whilst being alive and living with the family. He explained to Dick that he purposefully played that specific role to demonstrate to Dick the type of person that he should not become or grow up to be one day. Dick cried as he relayed the story to Kate and later confirmed that she was right all along, his dad was not a bad person at all. Kate was very fond of his dad after meeting him and never picked up any bad energy from him. Kate made this known to Dick but could not convince him otherwise as she had only met the man on very few occasions and for short periods of time. As she did not live with the man or know the details of what Dick and his family lived through with him, Dick didn't appreciate Kate's sense of him. The story was extremely emotional, and Kate got a sense that Dick had finally gained closure and forgave his dad during the reading, and he had finally made peace with his dad's actions whilst here on earth.

Dick's guides and angels also came through and went on to confirm that Kate and Dick were brother and sister in soul terms during this life and past lives too. In fact, in one lifetime, they were even twins. This would explain why Dick and Kate lacked chemistry and the intimacy of husband and wife. The contract that they entered in the spirit world was long expired, and their relationship should have ended a long time ago. The lady did not give any details of the actual contract, but confirmed that Dick was correct in wanting the divorce. She confirmed that Kate and Dick would have been successful with the new fertility doctor, and had Dick decided not to follow through with the divorce, then they would have fell pregnant with twins. This would have just prolonged the divorce, which was inevitable and would have been much harder for both because of the children. She went onto to say that both Kate and Dick were not intended to have kids in this lifetime. In a short space of time following the divorce, Kate would move on as she was to meet someone who had already been in her life.

Kate's only response to Dick was if they were brother and sister in soul terms, and knew this subconsciously or before having chosen this life, why would they have chosen a relationship of husband and wife roles this time round? Dick explained that they were meant to learn specific life lessons from each other, and this was the main reason for coming together.

The reading gave Dick comfort and confirmation of this big decision that he had to make.

Kate made her way to the conference with a colleague and, as she drove, she processed all that had transpired in the last few hours. Dick messaged her during the day to check if she was doing okay. No one around her had any idea of what was going on in her head or the news that had just been broken to her. Kate was calm and well composed, at least on the surface.

Kate had a few physiological reactions to the news over the next two to three days. This included symptoms such as nausea, a lack of appetite, a feeling of a deep void in her stomach, tiredness and insomnia. She had felt as though a train had run over her.

Whilst Dick dropped a bombshell on Kate after having months to reflect and decide, it was now time for Kate to reflect and digest. She needed to accept the reality she was faced with, and she needed to ask herself a few important questions. More importantly, she needed to be honest with herself. When she asked herself the question whether she was happy, she realised that she was only about fifty percent happy. She lived her life for everyone but herself. Dick was priority – making him happy, doing things that would please him and his family. She constantly tried to keep the peace; she craved his affirmation and affection and was really lost.

Kate quickly realised that if she was only about fifty per-cent happy, then she had a lot to gain with this newfound free-dom. Dick had essentially offered her a second chance at life! This was the greatest gift she could have asked for! Kate started to change her perspective and how she viewed and responded to Dick's decision. She started to look at the positives and the underlying blessings. Her greatest blessings and protec-tion were not being successful with the fertility treatment. She would have dedicated her life and continued sacrificing herself for their child or children. She now had been given the greatest gift ever by Dick: freedom, peace and a chance to live again!

In less than forty-eight hours, Kate accepted the divorce. Her story was different; the negative connotations associated with divorce were not going to put a damper on her spirit. In her case, a divorce from Dick meant a new beginning, a sense of enlightenment, freedom, peace, and finally accepting herself for who she truly was.

Kate decided to work from home for the next two days due to her inability to sleep. She was struggling with insomnia and was tired at this stage.

The following day when Dick left to work, Kate decided to share the news with Maria. Whilst she had only been working for Kate and Dick for just over six months, Maria had formed a close bond with Kate, the sisterly type. Maria was shocked and heartbroken. She broke down crying, and her immediate reaction was that Kate should not accept it and fight to make it work. Kate had to explain to her that Dick had decided that the marriage was over for them, and she had no choice but to accept it, strengthen herself for what lay ahead and prepare to move on. Kate shared with Maria in the months to come the struggles and difficult relationship she and Dick shared.

Kate messaged Dick's best friend, and to her surprise, he had not yet been told the news by Dick. Kate didn't get into any of the details, but explained that Dick was going to be going through a challenging time, and she wanted his commitment and reassurance that he would be there to support Dick. Even though Dick had made this decision, Kate was nonetheless concerned that he did not have a support network as she did.

Over the next two days, Kate took the time to absorb the information and reflect. She also aimed to build up her strength and the courage to tell her parents. Given that they were her parents, she knew that naturally they would be shocked and feel immense hurt and sadness for her. As a result, she chose not to share the story from a point of weakness.

Kate decided to share the news with her parents separately. She asked her mum over to her place. When she arrived, her mum found it strange that Kate was at home, but believed that there was, of course, a good reason that she must be working from home! Kate's mum did not have the slightest idea of the news that was to come! Kate began by telling her that she needed to share something with her, but first she needed for her to sit right beside her. Kate reassured her mum that what she was going to share with her would naturally hurt her, and she would feel pain as Kate was her child and she only ever wants the best for Kate. However, she needed to know that Kate was accepting of it and everything in time would be ok.

Kate told her mum what had happened, and that Dick had asked for a divorce. She was completely at a loss for words as she did not see this one coming at all! Kate then had to give her context and went into the details of what she had experienced in the prior twelve years of knowing Dick and her relationship with him. This made it easier for Kate to explain why she was so accepting of his decision and why she felt this was an opportunity for her to get a second chance at life. Kate's mum kept asking why she did not share any of the challenges with them. Kate had to explain that she was an adult, and she had to go through her battles and her own lessons. Whilst initially, Kate would share everything with her mum, she came to the realisation and found out the hard way that her mum would naturally take her side and sympathise more with Kate.

Kate never wanted anyone to have a negative perception about Dick, and so she never bad-mouthed him to her parents or family.

Kate's mum was convinced that Dick's family, more specifically his mother, had something to do with this because just two weekends prior, Dick had driven down to Durban alone with his family for his aunt's funeral. Kate's mum was sure that Kate and Dick's relationship was discussed during the trip, contributing to Dick's decision. Kate had to reassure her that none of this really mattered; the actual status of their relationship was such regardless.

Kate's mum then shared that they used to observe the way that Dick spoke to her and addressed her at times, but because Kate was accepting of being spoken to in this manner, everyone just left it.

Kate acknowledged that this was a choice she had made: to not stand up for herself. As time went along and she matured as a person, she started to stand up to Dick and fight for what she believed in. Kate allowed Dick to dominate and control her. The turning point was after Dick's sister's wedding and the endless issues, Kate had begun speaking her mind without any fear of how Dick would react.

Kate and her mum also discussed how Kate's niece and nephew were going to handle the news, as they were both very close to Dick, more so Kate's nephew who absolutely idolised Dick! Kate and Dick had already discussed that they would tell the kids together. Kate also shared with her mum that Dick had said that both dogs could remain with her, as Titus was extremely attached to her. Although Leah was new, she had already formed a bond with Titus and her. Dick insisted that he would pay maintenance for the dogs as they were like his own children! Kate and her mum tightly hugged each other and had a small cry. They then messaged Kate's dad to come over so that she could share the news with him.

Kate's dad, on the other hand, suspected that there was something wrong for sure. He thought that Kate either wanted to ask him for financial assistance with the new fertility treatment or that Kate and Dick were going to separate. Kate found the latter quite surprising.

There are very few occasions that Kate had ever seen her dad come to tears or cry. The once was when Kate and Dick left for Bermuda, and the second time was when Kate told him about the divorce. Unlike Kate's mum, Kate witnessed a wave of emotions go through him, from immense sadness to anger, hurt and pain. Then he started cursing saying that if Dick's mother had anything to f*#king do with this, he would go and destroy them!

It appeared that Kate's dad and mum were on the same wavelength! Kate could understand that after all the past experiences with Dick's mother and his family, her parents would not put anything past them. They witnessed Kate not being treated as a daughter or part of Dick's family and strongly believed that Dick's mother would rather see the couple apart than together.

Kate shared the same brief with her dad as she had done with her mum. Her dad's reaction was the same – how could Kate not have told them about all the pain and difficulties that she was going through! Kate had to reassure him that not all her experiences were negative or bad, and it was all part of her growth and development and shaped her into the lady she had become. Dick played his role in that he took care of her and provided for her as his wife. Kate was working and equally contributed to their lifestyle and standards of living. She was ever short of nothing in the material sense.

Kate again explained to her dad that this was the best outcome for her and that she would be far better off on her own. She had a second opportunity at life! Kate's dad, being old school, was afraid of what people were going to say and how they would react to the news. Kate was not ashamed at all to let people know that she was divorced. In her case, the outcome was positive. Kate suggested that she take care of any comments or questions so that her dad did not need to feel awkward.

Kate's parents insisted that she return home to stay with them. Her dad told her that her bedroom at home was still open and available! Kate had to tell them that she was a grown woman and would be okay on her own but would reach out if needed. This, of course, was a very kind gesture and expected of parents; however, Kate needed her space and the time to reflect and figure things out.

Kate was relieved that things went as well as they could go with her parents. Dick had requested to meet them as well with Kate. They decided to give it some time, as Kate knew that her parents really required the time to digest and process the information too.

The next day Kate's parents hosted a prayer at their home, and Kate turned up alone. Everyone kept asking Kate where Dick was, but she was not yet ready to share her news with the extended family.

The following weekend, Kate signed up for an acrylic art course. That Saturday morning, she received a message from Dick, saying that her mum had messaged him asking him why things had to be this way and why he was doing this. Kate was upset that her mum had messaged him directly, because her mum knew that Kate had offered to answer absolutely any question related to the divorce. It was evident that the news was proving difficult for Kate's parents to accept as a reality.

At the end of the art course on the Sunday afternoon, Kate drove straight to her sister's place to share the news with her and her husband. If Kate thought her mum was at a loss for words, well her sister was completely silenced! She just sat there and did not say a word whilst her brother-in-law asked all the questions. He asked whether Dick and her would consider counselling. He was unaware that they had already done it twice before and, besides, Dick had not given Kate a choice this time, she was told that he wanted out.

The three of them agreed that they would wait for Kate's niece to complete her end-of-year school exams before sharing the news with her and Kate's nephew.

The following day, Kate's sister messaged her to say that she was sorry that she did not say anything, but she was really in such shock and completely thrown off!

The next few weeks at work were busy as Kate was on the road and out auditing suppliers. She enjoyed the change of scenery and being out of the office on her own, music on and just driving.

Dick's sister contacted Kate and wanted to arrange to see her. She assured Kate that she and her husband were also there to help Kate, and they wanted to support both her and Dick through this. Kate decided she was not ready to meet her, and perhaps one day she would be able to share her story with Dick's sister. She said she was very sorry for what Kate was going through and checked in now and again to see how Kate was doing. It was quite strange that after Dick had decided that he wanted a divorce and Kate was no longer a part of the family, his sister actually ended up being so kind, caring and concerned about Kate's well-being. Yet, none of this behaviour occurred whilst Kate was a sister-in-law!

Dick's brother called Kate, but she had missed his call. They later chatted on WhatsApp, and he said that he and his family were there for Kate and could not imagine what she was going through!

Kate did not hear a single word from Dick's mother – not a phone call, not a message. Why was she so surprised? Although their relationship was estranged over the years, she still expected Dick's mother, as a divorced female, to show some sort of empathy toward her and say something along the lines of *sorry to hear the news*. After knowing Dick's family for twelve years, Dick's mother's behaviour was confirmation of the way Kate had been treated all along: She was never a daughter in that family.

On his own, Dick contacted Kate's mum to ask when they could all meet. This was against Kate's wishes. She wanted to give her parents time to digest the news. Kate was extremely upset with Dick, but eventually it was arranged for him to meet with her parents. The purpose of the visit was for Dick to apologise for the hurt and pain, to say goodbye, and to thank them for all the support over the years. Dick said that he wanted to maintain relationships with certain of Kate's family members.

If they had to bump into each other anywhere, he did not want it to be awkward. Kate's parents did not say much to Dick besides that they treated him like a son in their house and, of course, that they were sad about what was decided. However, Kate and Dick had made up their minds. It was short and went smoothly and, for that, Kate was grateful.

The following weekend, albeit the third weekend after requesting the divorce, Dick was already wanting to discuss the paperwork for the divorce and for the sale of their house. It all seemed to be very rushed to Kate. She could not understand what the rush was about. She was still assimilating all this information and was definitely not going to change her mind, but Dick seemed to be very pushy. They sat down, and Dick explained to her that he had researched an online service that would make it really simple and easy to go through the formal paperwork process. He wanted to keep the house, if Kate was okay with this!

Kate was so overwhelmed by all of it. She could not believe how quickly he wanted it closed out, and she was not comfortable with him keeping the house. This was her dream house that he fought so hard to obtain for her, and she could not comprehend how he would want to live in it with someone else in the future! Kate said she would think about it and let him know.

The next morning before Kate could give him an answer, Dick said that she was right. He had decided that he no longer wanted the house. It was at this very moment that Kate had this burning urge inside of her. Before she knew it, she had sputtered out if there was a third party involved and whether this was the reason behind the rush with everything.

Dick immediately went on the defence and asked how Kate could even think that of him. Kate explained that it was natural for her to ask given his behaviour. Kate's mind was working overtime. She was trying to figure out who could it be at work that had ignited a spark within Dick. A girl came to mind. Dick would often mention her name to Kate, which was fine. However, Kate remembered him describing her as erotic and wanting to set her up with his best friend. She also recalled that Dick had told her that she was studying for her MBA. When Kate first met her, she thought this would be common ground and would make conversation easier, but this was not the case. Kate also cast her mind back to Dick's previous year-end work function. Kate felt extremely uncomfortable and out of place. This girl sat two seats away from Kate, and she and her friend did not even greet Kate or speak to her even though she had met Kate before. When they got home that evening, Kate mentioned to Dick that his friends were not very friendly towards her. Kate suspected that this person could be the third party.

That evening when Kate came home from work, she found Dick waiting for her, seated on the couch with luggage at his feet. He said to Kate that he had decided that it was not working out with him still staying in the house, and that he was leaving and would be staying at his mom's place. Exactly thirteen days after asking for the divorce, Dick left home.

Kate was shocked again as it was sudden but, as with all things, the decision was made by Dick. She had a very close childhood friend that she was meeting that evening, so she did not even begin to think about what this actually meant for her.

Kate and Dick's house was extremely large; the plot expanded one thousand five hundred square meters. Whilst there was an electric fence around the property, and an alarm system and cameras outside on the street, it was not the ideal situation for Kate to be living alone. Dick, in fact, took a long time to adjust to the new surroundings and sounds when they moved into the house. Yet, he was quite comfortable leaving Kate on her own when there had been two attempted neigh-bouring burglaries just the week before.

That evening after Kate's friend left, she said to herself, *I am always protected, and I have absolutely nothing to worry about!* Moreover, from that day on, Kate stayed alone on the property with the dogs. She never lost a wink of sleep and was not afraid at all. Kate did not tell her family that Dick had moved out, because they would have been worried about her being alone in the house. Her brother-in- law later found out via Dick that he had moved out and that Kate was alone there.

No one at work knew what Kate was going through. She finally started to share with the girls that she worked closely with. They were shocked at what had transpired and that she was handling everything so well. Employees from other departments randomly commented about how much brighter Kate was looking in her face, that she seemed more relaxed, and as though a heavy weight was no longer pulling her down. People around her noticed the physical change and transformation that was taking place without the full context or background.

Kate received the following letter emailed to her from Dick on the 5th November, a week and a half after he left home:

To my Dear Kate,

It's 3:44am on Thursday the 5th of November when I have started writing this. There hasn't been a night where I have been away where I don't think of you and the pain I've caused. Even though I know it is the right decision, it doesn't make it easy. Seeing you hurting and angry last night is hurting me and what's worse is that I have caused it.

I have just woken up from a dream that has affected me greatly and decided to write this letter. I hope that you will read it and it will put things in perspective. When I went to the medium, she said my female guide has a beautiful smile with the most amazing voice. It's weird as I have always found female singers soothe me, like Dido and Jewel. I have been very down and depressed lately because of the way you feel. I knew that this would happen but yet my connection with you is strong and the compassion will always be there. In my dream last night, you and I went to an event, at the event Céline Dion came and sat next to us. You however did not react to her the way I did. Celine sat near me, next to you and took my hand. She looked at me and I was overwhelmed with emotion and gratitude. She held my hands tightly and comforted me. Every time that I tried to tell her about you and how much you love her she ignored me. Instead, all she wanted me to do was to be comforted by her and it was like she knew exactly what I was feeling and wanted me to know that she is there and everything will be ok.

I know that this will be extremely difficult for you and I can't imagine what you are going through. We've always known that chemistry between us never really existed. There is a deep compassionate bond between us but not an intimate one. Since when we first got married, I used to tell you that there's no honeymoon period. A man and a woman who've saved themselves for marriage should want nothing more than to consume each other. That has never happened. I have even mentioned how you and I feel like brother and sister. This has been a constant issue that we speak about every year. This year has been no different. It's exceptionally important that you understand that this is not about sex, it's about passion and intimate connection. It's about being able to drive in a car and your partner has their hand on your lap. It's about being in an exotic location or a holiday and all you can do when alone is be intimate with each other. It's about being in any part of your house and making passionate love to each other irrespective of the setting. It's about those deep kisses, French kisses where it doesn't feel awkward, because all you want is more and more of your partner. I have always dreamed of it and that dream has not materialised even though we have tried, and I have found myself giving up on it. I have given it all the time that I can and unfortunately time has caught up with me.

Intimacy is the most important part of me. I would give up many, if not all, of your perfect traits to have someone who has that connection with me. Someone who I don't have to look across at every time I laugh to see if they enjoy the same humour that I do and realise that the joke does not feel as good because you can't enjoy it with me, the same as me. Someone who will want to rip my clothes off, appreciate the body I have and want to stay in bed with me for a weekend and do nothing else than stay at home with me under blankets watching TV and making love. Someone who wants me physically and intensely, the way I want them.

I know you are angry with me because we have built this life together and now, I have destroyed it. I am also angry with you because you don't understand what I have been through and most importantly what I've sacrificed for all these years and why I have come to this decision. Please be clear that I'm not saying these years are wasted, I'm saying that I've tried my best to suppress the most important love language I have so that you, and ultimately, we, could be happy. I need you to understand that as a man, I have needs and desires and I have tried to satisfy those with you, but after over 9 years as a devoted and faithful husband, and most importantly, a passionate man, it has not come to fruition.

I have constantly prayed (whenever I felt down about this) that you find someone who brings that out of you so that you could leave me and we can move on. I know that I would take it much better than you and it would be easier for us. Even when you spent your time with Ed, I used to ask you if you think he is the one and I would have been fine if you had left me for him. With what we were going through at the time, a part of me hoped that you would leave me for him so that you would find what you wanted, and I could look for what I needed. Unfortunately, that is not the way this life was set out. That is the easy way out and I need to make the hard decision. Like you said to William, we need to be responsible for our own happiness. As such I would need to break the heart of the person, I care the most for. The person I have grown the most with. The person I respect the most. The most amazing person I have met. Unfortunately, a relationship cannot last when that person is fulfilled (and possibly you are not) and the other is not. My love tank is at least half empty and the most perfect life that we have surrounded ourselves by does not fill it. The dream house, gorgeous dogs, cinema room, gym, cars, figurines, financial stability, promise of children, all don't satisfy an emptiness that I have, one which we together cannot fill. We have tried and we have given it more than the time it deserves to see if it is there, and unfortunately it isn't. In hindsight this decision should have been made back when we went for counselling, but we tried again. Now it is more complicated due to what we have filled our lives with.

I want you to know that I have never and would never be unfaithful to you. That is not the man I am, and you know that. It breaks my heart to see you the way you are, knowing that this will be the most important decision of my life and the worst moment of yours (for now, I believe it will change in time). We both need to live our life of truth. I need to be honest with myself and you.

I interact with people every day and wish that I could have those same interactions with you. I wish that you would get me like other people do, understand my passions and share in it. We have both grown with each other. We are better people today than they were when we met each other. We have both helped each other to grow to a point, a climax. You need to find the person that brings that passion out of you, and I need to do the same. Life is all about passion.

I also believe in the signs that led up to this decision. They have been strong as I have mentioned. You telling me that I don't have to be responsible for you and that you can take care of yourself. Saying that you love Titus more than me. The fact that our infertility was misdiagnosed. The lack of intimacy during the Cancun holiday (and all other holidays). The lack of intimacy in our dream house. The medium was only a confirmation of the most important decision I had already decided to make. When you know you're going to hurt the most important person in your life, you would want some sort of confirmation. I also know that you have gone to see someone but you have never spoken to me about it so I don't know what you've found out. I hope that that person brought comfort to you.

I need you to set me free. I need you to understand what I have been going through and what my reasoning is and most importantly, I need to set you free. I am and will always be amazed by the person you are. You have been so strong through this process, and I always underestimate how strong you are. You have always proved me wrong. You never cease to amaze me. You have so much beauty and you need to find the one who can unlock it further. You and I are not meant to be that for each other. We were meant to be the support we have been for each other (and hopefully continue to be for each other) which has grown us into better people. Through this process we will know what we need from our next partner and not sacrifice that which is most important to us.

You are deserving of love, and I never want you to forget that. I hope you find an intense love that someone will give you and bring out of you that will show you a different side to yourself. I hope that you let your guard down and give yourself completely and lose yourself in love.

As I've said, I will always love you. There is an eternal bond between us, and I don't want to lose that. But if you cannot forgive me for what I've done, I will make peace with it over time. My intention is not to hurt you but to live my truth and wish that you can live yours. My truth might not be right for you as your truth might not be right for me.

I will always be here for you whenever you need me.

I love you!

Each statement in this letter was Dick's perception, and it angered Kate. She really wanted to respond to let him know her perspective, but she decided it was not worth it. Not for a minute did he even think to consider her perspective, or even question why she was so accepting of the divorce. Did he think that she was blissfully happy, and he was the only unhappy one?

Weeks later, Kate's niece's exams were done, and she really wanted to share the news with them as they had to keep this "secret" going for a few months now. Each time she met them, including for her birthday, Kate had to tell a white lie as to where their uncle was.

That morning, Dick had a miscommunication with Kate on the time they had agreed to meet and talk because she had a hair appointment before. Therefore, they ended up not discussing what they were going to say to the kids, although Dick sent Kate a message before he arrived and summarised what he wanted to say. The message did not include using the word divorce. Kate did not think that she needed to spell this out to him, either, but she was not planning to use the term divorce.

Dick was extremely nervous upon arrival, Kate could tell. This was very unusual and out of character for him. Kate then suggested that they go out into the garden to play with the dogs. They spent time in the garden with the dogs and then later moved to the swimming pool as it was a very hot day. Eventually, Kate could see that Dick could not even begin to start chatting to the kids about the divorce. She decided that after all, it was her niece and nephew, so she would do it.

Kate began telling them that she and Dick were always really close as friends, but no longer had the feelings required to be married and that they had decided they would be going separate ways. The next thing, Dick interjected, "yes, your aunt and I are getting a divorce!" Kate was perturbed with his statement and asked him immediately why he needed to use the D word to explain! Her niece said it was fine; she knew what it meant because her friends' parents were divorced. Of course, Dick justified that he was correct in using the terminology.

Kate's nephew was only six at the time, and her niece was eleven, and she was afraid of how they would handle it. They were both very close to Dick, more so than his own brother's kids. They both immediately asked what would happen with their cousins Titus and Leah, and Dick reassured them that they would remain with their aunt. He also told them that once he got his new place, they could come and visit him at any time that they wished. They would still spend time with him, just not with him and their aunt.

After Kate had done the difficult part of breaking the news to the kids, Dick took over controlling the situation and making sure he still looked good in their eyes. Kate was done. She got up and decided to go and release the frustration that she felt and went for a run and workout.

Kate's niece joined her in the gym when she returned. Her niece was most definitely an old soul with a very empathic nature. In the saddest of moments, she would make an appropriate gesture or say something to someone just to lighten the situation. She turned around at this point and said to Kate that she should not worry about when she gets married next, as she would be her bridesmaid and her cousin's daughter would be the flower girl! This just made Kate's day! Her niece was already looking to the future, and said something to give Kate hope and make her feel lighter and uplifted in the moment! Kate also found it was quite strange, given that if the opportunity did arise for a second time around, she also most certainly had a white wedding in mind. This would be on point with the need for her niece to be a bridesmaid and the need to have a flower girl!

Although Dick used the word divorce, which was against Kate's wishes, she was proud of herself for handling the situation and starting out the conversation and delivering the main message in the most delicate way possible. The kids completely surprised Kate as they handled it way better than she expected!

On the drive home, Kate told the kids that they could call her at any time if they had any questions. Her nephew asked again, but why does this have to happen? Kate wished that there was an easier way in which to answer his question!

In preparation for her birthday, Kate planned a Saturday night out the weekend before with her friends. They all went for dinner and a night out dancing at her favourite nightclub. Kate had a fantastic time being free to dance and drink as much as she wanted to!

On the morning of her birthday, Kate was extremely emotional – it was the first year that she woke up to being entirely alone and just with her dogs. Maria arrived, and she brought Kate a gift and a card. This made her even more emotional, and she cried! Kate had the entire day planned, but it was most certainly different. Her phone was extremely busy as it always was on her birthday, and she was rushing to get done to go meet her parents for breakfast before a massage. She missed Dick's calls about three times, and this was not intentional at all. Eventually, she called him back whilst on her way to breakfast. Dick was sad and said that it was the worst day of his life! He could not imagine what she was going through. Kate reassured him that she was good, and it was her day to be celebrated! He even went as far as saying that maybe he should have waited until after her birthday to break the news to her. Kate found this strange because she felt this would have made things worse, him pretending whilst he knew what was to come!

When Kate returned home, she received an arrangement of flowers from Dick. They were white, green and purple. They immediately reminded her of a bouquet of flowers appropriate for a funeral or loss of a loved one! The message in the card read:

Dear Kate,

Happy Birthday!

Ho'oponopono - I love you. I am sorry. Please forgive me. Thank you.

Love Dick

Kate appreciated the gesture, but did not understand why he was asking for forgiveness as she was not holding anything against him. Was there something of which he was guilty?

Kate spent lunch with her sister, niece and nephew and was very moved by the card that her sister gave her. She expressed for the first time how proud she was of the woman that Kate had become and how much she loved her!

That evening, Kate went out for dinner with her friends. They had much laughter and fun! Kate thoroughly enjoyed her day!

Kate had a friend that was a lawyer, and so she asked her for a contact for a good divorce attorney. Dick had been very quiet on the progress of the divorce papers. So, Kate made an appointment as she wanted to be proactive and ready once Dick served her with a settlement agreement. Well, this ironically turned out to be an extremely long process after him saying that there was a simple quick fix. Dick decided to use the legal insurance component to their normal insurance policy. This would normally be used for small cases that you may require legal advice/assistance for, but certainly was not appropriate for a divorce case. Kate was very glad though that they had at least one lawyer that was well versed in the process and advised the most streamlined way to deal with their case. Already from the onset, Dick's lawyer wanted to issue a summons to Kate as opposed to first drawing up a settlement agreement which they would sign. This would mean that Kate's lawyer would need to defend her, which was unnecessary, as they were not contesting the divorce. Once the ball got rolling, it was summer holidays, and not much was done from Dick's side. So, they went through December without a signed agreement.

A few days before Christmas, Dick came over to meet Kate's niece and nephew to give them their Christmas presents. Kate never really made eye contact with him when he came over to the house, but this time everyone, including Kate's mum, could not help but wonder what on earth was going on! Dick was always clean-shaven, but he had grown an entire beard! Even her nephew commented and asked him if he was growing old because he was not gyming! They all burst out laughing! Kids do say the most innocent of things!

Kate arranged for Dick's nieces' gifts to be ready as well which she sent back with him. She was quite disappointed, once again, that she only received a message from his brother to say thank you, but not even a phone call to allow the twins to speak to her once they opened their gifts.

A friend of Kate's invited a few of their friends to her place for New Year's Eve. Kate was going to stay over the night at her friend's place, and so Dick decided to stay at the house with the dogs. Kate felt sorry for Dick because it seemed as though he had no plans, not even with his family. New Year's Eve was always a time that was spent with family and friends. Kate felt a bit anxious in the afternoon and fearful for what lay ahead in the New Year. She decided to take some time to reflect and make note of the lessons and highlights that she had experienced over the past year.

Kate then got ready and had a great night out with her friends. She sent Dick a nice New Year's message wishing him all the very best for the new year ahead. Kate was not sure whether Dick would have necessarily wished her, but because she sent a message, he responded also wishing her well. When Dick saw her the next day though, he laughed and asked, why don't they hug and wish each other properly for New Years? That made Kate feel awkward, wishing each other over the phone was one thing, but she was really not ready to hug and wish him in person!

CHAPTER 12
The Lighter Side of Her

As a young girl ... Kate was very much a tomboy! She spent a lot of time with her dad watching sports, and weekends were filled with many hours of watching cricket, be it one-day internationals or an entire test match, spending five days without missing a single ball. Kate and her dad would be glued to the television, with only time for quick bio breaks. They were spoilt and waited on by her mum, with delicious food served throughout.

Kate's childhood hero and man crush was of course none other than Jonathan Neil Rhodes, well-known to the rest of the world as Jonty. Little did she know that this great fantasy would one day become a reality when she was afforded numerous opportunities to personally meet Jonty face-to-face. This became a routine, whether it be at airports, stadiums or marketing events. Wherever Jonty was, Kate was there! This is the time during which her attraction towards men with blonde hair and blue eyes began.

Kate's dad always wanted the best for his family and, thus, allowed her the opportunity to attend a semi-private school also known as a Model C school, and what do you know?! It was a sea of boys with blonde hair and blue eyes. Later in high school, Kate was the cricket scorer for the first XI team. This meant travelling with a bus full of boys, and Kate was the only girl; it meant being a boy magnet with all these boys depending on Kate for their run rates, bowling figures and match statistics. Moreover, this is where her attention was drawn to Mark.

Mark was not blonde, but he sure had the blue eyes. He was well built, charismatic, a prefect and all that a 16-year-old girl could dream of in a boy! Kate fancied Mark, but sadly, it was one-sided. Well, so she thought. Kate would generously give Mark her science homework to copy just because he was Mark, and she thought that somehow perhaps he would notice her a little bit more. She was keen on getting his attention!

In 1998, the school hosted the annual Valentine's ball, and Kate wished for nothing more than for Mark to ask her to the ball as his partner. This never materialised, but she was given one slow dance with him. The song was "With Or Without You" by U2. This was the perfect moment for Kate. She was extremely nervous, her heart was pounding, her palms were clammy, and she couldn't help but wonder if he felt the same for her in that moment. Was he dancing with a friend, or could he possibly be thinking of her as someone other than just a friend? Kate could feel the heat between them as Mark held his arms around her waist; this was as far as it went, three minutes of slow dancing and nothing more.

After high school, Mark moved to Australia, and they lost contact for a few years. Seven years later, Kate and Mark reconnected through social networking. However, by then Kate was already married to Dick and Mark was nothing more than an unspoken high school crush that had faded. Kate and Mark's chats were far and few in between as life had moved on.

It was in the middle of December 2015 – just less than two months after Dick had asked Kate for the divorce – that she received a message from Mark. He shared that he had dreamt about her and was just making contact to say hi and see how she was doing. Kate found this surreal as no one besides her close friends and family knew about the divorce. Kate responded expressing her surprise in him making contact, given her current circumstances and what she was going through. She shared her news of the divorce, and Mark empathised with her and asked if she was still in love with Dick. Of course, she would always have a deep love for Dick, but with all that had transpired, she could not find any more tears to shed for him. Mark thought Kate deserved better. He reassured her that she was young, strong, intelligent, gorgeous and hot and could start all over again if she wanted to. The conversation continued for a while, and he was very encouraging. Kate was flattered with all the compliments she was receiving from Mark, as her level of confidence had been on a low for many years. He said he could tell from her writing that she knew what she needed to do to move forward and that she was mentally strong. Mark had married in 2013 and had a baby boy. She kept wondering where Mark's wife was given that he had been online chatting to her for quite some time. A few hours passed by and unexpectedly he texted:

2015/12/12, 9:41:24 PM: Mark: I miss you

2015/12/12, 9:41:38 PM: Mark: I was a bit of a dick at school I think

2015/12/12, 9:42:00 PM: Kate: Lol

2015/12/12, 9:42:08 PM: Kate: And now u married and all grown up

2015/12/12, 9:45:24 PM: Kate: Do u remember the v day ball

2015/12/12, 9:45:45 PM: Mark: They are both grown up

2015/12/12, 9:45:55 PM: Kate: 😄

2015/12/12, 9:46:19 PM: Mark: I remember

2015/12/12, 9:48:21 PM: Mark: You wanted to dance with me to that one song

2015/12/12, 9:48:33 PM: Mark: What was it again?

2015/12/12, 9:48:42 PM: Kate: U2

2015/12/12, 9:48:58 PM: Kate: Can't remember the title

2015/12/12, 9:52:42 PM: Mark: I remember the slow dance but I don't remember the song

2015/12/12, 9:53:04 PM: Mark: I was wearing those ridiculous yellow tinted shades

2015/12/12, 9:55:55 PM: Kate: Lol yes

2015/12/12, 9:56:05 PM: Kate: I think I have a photo

2015/12/12, 9:56:09 PM: Kate: Must look for it

2015/12/12, 9:56:49 PM: Mark: No please don't look for it ha ha

Kate rummaged through her stuff and managed to find the photo and sent it to him. She also found several of their photos from when they went away on school camps. She felt a sense of nostalgia as she fondly looked back at the old memories.

2015/12/12, 10:13:50 PM: Mark: You know I liked you right?

Kate was convinced he was drunk! There was no way he could have liked her in high school.

2015/12/12, 10:16:06 PM: Kate: Nope I didn't

2015/12/12, 10:16:50 PM: Mark: Looking back I was a dick

2015/12/12, 10:16:59 PM: Mark: The cool kids and all

2015/12/12, 10:17:23 PM: Kate: Lol don't be hard on yourself

2015/12/12, 10:17:31 PM: Kate: I was an ugly duckling 😂😂

2015/12/12, 10:20:38 PM: Mark: I really did like you a lot. I think you knew that after I sent that message on tickertape

Now Kate was confident he was drunk!

2015/12/12, 10:20:57 PM: Mark: My mum still talks about you ha ha

2015/12/12, 10:21:21 PM: Kate: What msg?

2015/12/12, 10:21:27 PM: Kate: Lol was just gonna ask how is ur mum

2015/12/12, 10:25:27 PM: Mark: Don't you remember sending

me ticker timer letters

2015/12/12, 10:27:23 PM: Mark: Remember in science class we had to do those time versus velocity etc

2015/12/12, 10:27:42 PM: Mark: I used to write on the letters to you

2015/12/12, 10:27:41 PM: Kate: Yeah

2015/12/12, 10:28:23 PM: Kate: Lol u were just a douche that didn't reciprocate and now tells me all this so many years later

2015/12/12, 10:28:46 PM: Mark: No

2015/12/12, 10:28:56 PM: Mark: You know why

2015/12/12, 10:29:03 PM: Mark: And it's bad

2015/12/12, 10:29:26 PM: Kate: Nope I don't

2015/12/12, 10:29:29 PM: Kate: Do tell me

2015/12/12, 10:29:33 PM: Mark: I thought people would tease us because of our race

2015/12/12, 10:29:37 PM: Kate: Lol

2015/12/12, 10:29:47 PM: Mark: And now I look at it and it's so stupid

2015/12/12, 10:29:55 PM: Kate: Yeah I guess back in the day it wasn't that accepted

2015/12/12, 10:30:01 PM: Mark: But back then I was just a stupid kid

2015/12/12, 10:30:07 PM: Kate: Now people don't see colour

2015/12/12, 10:30:17 PM: Mark: And worried about what the cool kids thought

2015/12/12, 10:30:34 PM: Kate: 😂 who were the cool ones

2015/12/12, 10:30:40 PM: Mark: When there was such a cool girl sitting right next to me

2015/12/12, 10:31:43 PM: Mark: Just you were great and you still are

2015/12/12, 10:31:50 PM: Mark: Better than most

2015/12/12, 10:32:10 PM: Kate: Ahh u don't know how much it all means to me

2015/12/12, 10:32:17 PM: Kate: Especially now

2015/12/12, 10:33:03 PM: Kate: In the beginning when this all happened, I wondered how I wud move on and then when I started going out with friends I've had many guys just come up and chat to me and buy me a drink

2015/12/12, 10:33:18 PM: Kate: So it's all been great for my confidence

2015/12/12, 10:33:31 PM: Kate: When u in such a long relationship u forget urself

2015/12/12, 10:34:23 PM: Kate: Btw all the attention I've been getting going out is from white guys, so maybe I will finally meet my white guy and live happily ever after

2015/12/12, 10:35:04 PM: Kate: U know growing up I always had this dream of getting married in a white dress

2015/12/12, 10:35:18 PM: Kate: When it didn't happen, I was like oh well

2015/12/12, 10:35:28 PM: Kate: Now it cud still happen 😆

2015/12/12, 10:35:57 PM: Mark: You are hot

2015/12/12, 10:36:00 PM: Mark: Gorgeous

2015/12/12, 10:36:18 PM: Mark: I used to stare at you in science class

2015/12/12, 10:36:24 PM: Kate: Lol

2015/12/12, 10:36:32 PM: Kate: When I came to Australia we didn't meet

2015/12/12, 10:36:37 PM: Kate: Was it cos I was married?

2015/12/12, 10:36:56 PM: Mark: You didn't tell me you were here silly

2015/12/12, 10:37:01 PM: Kate: I did

2015/12/12, 10:37:09 PM: Kate: That's how I have ur number

2015/12/12, 10:37:26 PM: Kate: We were communicating then u cudnt make it

2015/12/12, 10:37:31 PM: Kate: Only saw Heather

2015/12/12, 10:37:44 PM: Mark: Really? Oh Shit I must have fucked that up

2015/12/12, 10:37:51 PM: Kate: Lol

2015/12/12, 10:38:02 PM: Kate: Eish dodged me again

2015/12/12, 10:48:24 PM: Mark: Well now you are single

2015/12/12, 10:48:33 PM: Mark: You can find that white boy

2015/12/12, 10:51:25 PM: Mark: I'm sorry. I get really busy and then I shut things off

2015/12/12, 10:51:38 PM: Kate: For sure actually he will find me

2015/12/12, 10:51:44 PM: Kate: That's ok

2015/12/12, 10:51:50 PM: Kate: Gonna sleep now

2015/12/12, 10:51:56 PM: Kate: Chat again soon

2015/12/12, 10:51:58 PM: Kate: Night

2015/12/12, 10:52:41 PM: Mark: Sleep tight

Although it seemed like a case of odd timing, it was a great confidence booster for Kate knowing that the person that she had a crush on in high school confirmed after all these years that he also felt the same about her. It would have been great to have had this confirmed in high school; however, it was still positive to have him confirm how he perceived her back then and still now so many years later. All Kate yearned for was the affirmation.

Mark later joined his family in South Africa for their vacation, but would still text Kate in-between. At the time, Kate could not understand the purpose and reason why the universe would reveal to her how Mark really felt about her all those years ago and, to some extent, why now given that he was married and had a son! The chats over the next few days became quite heated and intense. Whilst they were great, flattering and intriguing, her subconscious kept reminding her to stay clear of Mark's intentions, but the conversation kept flowing.

2015/12/21, 12:46:30 AM: Mark: Because I do fantasize about us

2015/12/21, 12:47:29 AM: Kate: Before u contacted me

2015/12/21, 12:47:33 AM: Kate: Or since?

2015/12/21, 12:47:49 AM: Mark: Before

2015/12/21, 12:47:52 AM: Mark: And since

2015/12/21, 12:48:15 AM: Mark: I think that we should have fucked at school

2015/12/21, 12:48:50 AM: Kate: Ok that cud explain the dream

2015/12/21, 12:49:35 AM: Kate: It's prob safer u in Australia and I don't meet u alone

2015/12/21, 12:49:37 AM: Kate: Lol

2015/12/21, 12:50:28 AM: Mark: Yes, probably

2015/12/21, 12:50:51 AM: Mark: Keep thinking of the contrast of our skins together

Mark's chats made Kate feel things that she had not felt before. She could not even begin to imagine what it would feel like if they were to meet in person. However, this was all just a tease, as nothing would materialise. Kate's integrity would not allow her to entertain any of this once she knew Mark's intentions.

2015/12/21, 12:56:52 AM: Mark: I think about you naked and I get hard

2015/12/21, 12:56:58 AM: Mark: Really hard

2015/12/21, 12:57:23 AM: Kates: Do u love ur wife

2015/12/21, 12:57:31 AM: Mark: I do

2015/12/21, 12:57:40 AM: Mark: But I want to Fuck you

2015/12/21, 1:03:39 AM: Kate: Have u had feelings like this for other women

2015/12/21, 1:03:59 AM: Mark: Not really like this

2015/12/21, 1:04:03 AM: Mark: I am a horny guy

2015/12/21, 1:04:11 AM: Mark: I've always been naughty

2015/12/21, 1:04:33 AM: Kate: I think most guys always want it more than women

Kate always thought that there was something wrong with her in terms of intimacy, as Dick and her had never chatted like this over text messages whilst dating or courting, let alone in the bedroom when they were finally married. Kate was made out to be a nun, although she really believed that she had her very own side to her still to be discovered, and so this was just the very beginning. Her body was on fire whenever she would talk to Mark. Kate imagined that this would hopefully happen soon with the right person that was single! But this was certainly a great start!

Mark certainly tested her sticking to her integrity. He asked her for naked photographs of herself and would graphically describe all the things that he fantasized about them. Kate was so afraid that his wife would find his phone and the chats, but he always reassured her that the chats were deleted after they were done talking. Kate did not want to get caught up or accused of anything by his wife or be the cause of a broken family. Kate could not wrap her head around the fact that Mark was married, on holiday with his family but lying on the couch at a ridiculous hour, chatting to her and masturbating, whilst his wife was in bed. It sounded bizarre, and Kate was the only one that could control the situation. Kate realised that clearly he was in a vulnerable stage in his marriage. She asked numerous questions to try to assess his circumstances, as Kate believed perhaps the universe had brought him into her life again for her to help him and assist him with his marriage. He did not really give too much detail besides mentioning that he liked sex a lot, and although he lived with his wife before marriage, she was very innocent, and he initiated a lot. His explanation could have been summarised as a lack of passion or fantasy he was experiencing, and Kate identified with it as this was like what she had experienced with Dick. It still did not make sense though, if he loved his wife as a best friend, why would he be fantasizing about a girl from high school more than a decade later?

Mark asked Kate how many guys she had been with. Kate had only slept with Dick as she had saved herself for marriage. Mark thought it would be great for Kate to enjoy sex with someone else. Indeed, Kate too wished for this moment in the future that she would enjoy having sex with a significant other!

Mark's intentions were very clear, as all he wanted to do if given the slightest opportunity to meet Kate, was to have passionate sex with her! The interaction, however, did make her realise that she could feel things that she never felt before. Kate was completely turned on by all his chats. He lifted her confidence and made her feel so sexy!

Mark persisted on the prospect of seeing Kate in early January, as he was in Johannesburg. Kate agreed that she would only meet with him if he brought his wife with him given all that he shared about how he felt. The meeting did not materialise, and he would message her saying that he could not believe how they could not just meet as adults and be mature about it. He would randomly message Kate at odd hours, even though he knew she was continuing with life and had met someone.

Later, in March, Kate went to Australia for a business trip, and Mark again attempted to meet her. Kate declined the chance to meet him. When she got back home, he messaged her to find out if she had arrived safely and if they would ever meet. Kate responded with honesty, and all she could say was that given his circumstances and all that he shared with her, she really did not know whether this was ever going to materialise! This was the last that Kate heard from Mark.

CHAPTER 13
Falling Into You

In primary school, Kate's best friend was Rebecca. The girls lost contact for a few years and then reconnected on Facebook in 2007. It was great, as they could see what had been happening in each other's lives. Rebecca, ironically, got married on Kate and Dick's 5th wedding anniversary. Kate contacted Rebecca through Facebook, and they would chat now and again, but never got around to making a date to see each other. In recent years, Kate had a strong urge to meet Rebecca. Kate picked up from Facebook that Rebecca had changed her surname back to her maiden name, and she was unsure how to ask her what had happened. After Dick had asked for the divorce, Kate messaged Rebecca and they met for dinner.

It was great catching up with her, and it was so strange how their life experiences were paralleled in so many aspects. Kate now had a sounding board and someone that she could openly share everything with. Rebecca had experienced the same first-hand, and Kate was extremely grateful to have connected with her again and to have her back in her life.

Kate had spent three weeks at home during the December holidays, which were wonderful. It was restful and peaceful quality time alone with Titus and Leah. They would wake up late, and Kate would laze around in her pyjamas until lunchtime and then get going for the day. Kate's body needed the rest and the time to reflect.

By the start of the third week though, Kate was bored! She met Rebecca for lunch, and they got chatting about Tinder.

Kate was reluctant to join because of the negative things that she had heard about it. Rebecca, however, convinced her that it was a way for her to pass time, put herself out there again and connect with people. Therefore, they decided to set up Kate's account. Kate was conservative when it came to the age of men she was interested in, as she thought she should be setting this criterion at her age and above. Rebecca advised that she should set it from thirty years old and upwards! In terms of the geographical radius, again Rebecca advised that she should not limit herself, and got Kate to widen this to a fifty-kilometre radius rather than the twenty kilometres that she had chosen!

Tinder is linked to your Facebook profile, and the last few Facebook profile pictures are automatically drawn from there and set up as your profile. You can, however, change these as you wish. Kate was okay with the pictures that were loaded, as her profile pictures on Facebook were always just of herself alone without Dick.

Kate got home and decided to spend the afternoon scoping out Tinder and to explore what it was all about! Kate sat for hours just scrolling through profiles, and there were hardly any profiles that remotely interested her at all! You could instantly guess at those that were lying about their age. Certain profiles would have such poor-quality photos or photos that were so old that it would be difficult to know if the person still actually looked like that at all! Some had pictures with their previous partners, or could it be their current partners or potentially a sister... honestly there were all sorts! Others had pictures of them with their kids – well this one Kate was grateful for, because at least they could be eliminated immediately! Kate felt a bit anxious and concerned to think, *is this really the sea of options out there?! Come on, this cannot be it ...*

And then Kate came across a profile with pictures that were consistent. He had blonde hair, blue eyes, an adventurous pic, and his age was thirty (that would make him three years younger than Kate). His first picture had a slightly raised right eyebrow and a naughty smirk/grin, and she decided to swipe right! You have matched with Liam! Say something … type something …

So, Kate said *Hi* with a smiley face. It was ironic, because on both the criteria of age and radius, Kate would have missed matching with Liam if it was not for Rebecca's advice! Kate also matched with two other guys in the meantime, but Liam was by far the best she had seen that day. He did not respond to her message until later that evening.

Kate was nervous as this was the first time in twelve years that she was back out there and chatting to a guy! Nevertheless, it turned out to be so comfortable with Liam. Conversation just flowed, and they asked each other many questions. Not long into the chat, Liam asked Kate if she was married, as he noticed that she was wearing a red bindi! When Kate went back and looked at her profile pictures, indeed apart from her last profile picture, she wore a red bindi in all previous pictures used on her profile! Kate was really impressed with Liam's general knowledge and knowing the meaning of the red bindi.

So, early on, Kate shared her status with Liam. She was married for nine and a half years, but was in the process of getting divorced, and Dick had moved out of the house. He was sorry to hear this and hoped that all would go through easily for her with the least hassle. He also shared with her that he went through a similar experience … well, he was not married to the lady, but they had dated for five years. Out of the blue, she broke up with him. They were meant to move to Australia together, and would have possibly gotten married beforehand. Three months after breaking up with him, she had a new boyfriend on Facebook! When Kate asked him if he thought that she was seeing the guy whilst they were dating, he said he did not know. It would be a speculation, and he did not think he would want to know the answer in any case. Kate and Liam chatted on and asked general getting to know a person types of questions. Then, the following day, they decided it was probably easier to chat on WhatsApp, so Liam sent Kate his number.

Liam and Kate continued to chat every day, mostly in the evenings. Liam was back at work already for the New Year, and

Kate did not want to disturb him. She was extremely excited, though, as the conversations were really going well, and she had a good feeling about this! After a week, Kate's close girl-friends were telling her to ask him out for a drink so that they could meet in person to see if this was really what she wanted. They convinced Kate not to drag things out, as the smallest of his idiosyncrasies could put her off. So, Kate was brave enough and asked Liam if they could meet for a drink. He embarrass-ingly said that she had beat him to it, as he was going to ask.

Kate and Liam decided to meet on a Thursday evening after work. Kate got to choose the place, and she decided on a hotel bar that happened to be in very close proximity to Liam's work. The night before, Kate felt like an absolute teenager again, trying to decide what to wear and asking her girlfriends for assistance. Kate had a huge abrasion on her left leg from the knee downwards. – A few days prior, Titus had toppled her into the swimming pool, and her knee scraped against the leaf catcher and grazed the second step of the pool. Liam knew about the event, but she was still conscious of what the wound looked like as it was still very raw and sore. She eventually went with an outfit that she would feel most comfortable in.

Kate woke up the next morning and noticed that the gel polish had chipped off one of her toes – she needed to get that repaired before going to drinks after work! Kate wore a simple black pencil skirt that was knee length, and a black and white blouse that accentuated her waist. A plain black strappy high-heel sandal was chosen, and she finished the outfit off with sil-ver jewellery.

Kate was nervous and, at the same time, excited, the entire day at work. She could not stop talking about the drinks date that was just a few hours away. Kate and Liam messaged each other in the morning, and both were equally excited about the meeting after many hours of texting and talking over the phone.

Kate kept trying to remind herself that, as much as she needed to be herself and hope for the best, he also had to do the same. Kate shared that she was extremely nervous and if she was less talkative compared to what she had been like over the phone, Liam needed to understand that this was the first time in twelve years that she was doing this again!

It was the longest day at work that eventually came to an end. Kate went to get her nails fixed, and touched up her makeup in the car before making her way to the hotel. Kate left early enough to make sure that she would arrive before Liam, as she was afraid of walking into the bar and having to find him. In fact, she was an entire fifteen minutes early. Kate messaged him once she had parked and made her way inside, as Liam's offices were literally situated across the road.

Kate took deep breaths, but this still did not seem to help at all. Her heart was racing! She made her way inside and decided to sit at a chair at the bar. She could not wait any longer and decided to order a drink for herself and start sipping on it to calm her down! Gin and tonic coming up, ma'am!

Finally, Liam arrived, and exactly what Kate made sure to avoid, happened to him. She was sitting with her back facing the entrance through which Liam came through, and he was walking around trying to find her, whilst messaging to see where she was sitting. Kate stood up, and he sweetly leaned forward and hugged her when they greeted each other. Kate apologised for ordering her drink before he got there. Once he sat down and ordered his drink, Kate calmed down.

Conversation continued as it did over the phone, which Kate was really pleased about, and she did not seem too nervous once they began chatting. They discovered that Liam also worked at the bank during the time that Kate's dad was still at the bank, and so did Liam's dad! Liam seemed to have thought that Kate's face looked familiar, but he couldn't completely place her. Kate, however, did not recall his face. Liam's mannerisms did not bother Kate, he was well dressed, smelt good and he even had a tie on ... not for her, for work! But still! And she loved his socks ... he had on a pair of Paul Smith happy socks! They were extremely funky and said a lot about his personality!

Kate could not help but keep in the back of her mind

what Dick had brought up about the feeling of butterflies, and ensuring that there would be chemistry the next time round. Well, she did not feel butterflies when she saw Liam. So now what? They had two rounds of drinks, and it was time to leave. Kate had an early morning flight to Cape Town the next day, and Liam had a long drive to his parents' place.

Liam walked Kate to her car, and they both agreed it was good to have met each other. He hugged her goodbye, and said they would chat. He messaged later that evening saying it was wonderful to have met her, and Kate picked up that he seemed to be quite interested, more so than she was. Kate thought about it for a bit and then decided to just go with it until their first kiss, and then she would make up her mind about what she really wanted for them.

Kate's mum was staying over that evening so that she could take her to the airport the next morning. Kate imagined that it was probably a bit scary for her to think that Kate had already started attempting to get back out there. Kate reassured her mum that it was just a drink; she was not planning on getting married to the guy and they were just getting to know each other! Kate, too, did not expect to have met someone less than three months after Dick asking for the divorce.

It was difficult for Kate to wake up so early the next morning, but she was extremely excited as she was going to spend the weekend in Stellenbosch with very close friends. Kate had met these friends through Dick, and they used to spend a lot of time with them when the friends still lived in Johannesburg.

Kate and Liam continued chatting over WhatsApp throughout the weekend, and they would send pictures to each other of what they were doing. It was a while before they managed to arrange to see each other again, as Liam was a groomsman for one of his close mate's wedding that was coming up at the end of January. So, he was busy with wedding rehearsals, the bachelors, birthday parties, etc.

Liam had mentioned to Kate that he really wanted to kiss her after their first date when he was saying goodbye! Well, she was glad he did not because it may have just freaked her out a bit! They got into a discussion around this, as he wanted to know what Kate was comfortable with, since she was still in the process of the divorce. Kate shared that she was comfortable with seeing him, but that they just needed to be aware of being affectionate in public places in case someone she knew were to see them. Liam was happy with this, and said that he might consider kissing her on the cheek the next time he saw her.

Kate and Liam eventually arranged to meet for dinner one evening after work. It had been almost two weeks since the first time that they had met! The excitement and nerves were back, that was a good sign, and Kate was keen to see him again. Dinner was lovely! They had an awesome meal, and it was so good for Kate to be able to enjoy a glass of wine with a partner over a meal.

As Kate and Liam said goodbye to each other that evening, Liam went in really close to Kate and kissed her on the cheek. It felt really good, and then they hugged. Not too long after, Liam messaged to tell Kate that she smelt amazingly good.

Liam's friend's wedding was in two days' time, and then he had one day before he flew out to the UK for a week. When he arrived back from the UK, Kate was flying to Kenya for a week.

They both agreed from the beginning that they would only go with what made them both feel comfortable, and, learning from their previous relationships, they needed to be themselves.

Liam attended his friend's wedding and looked dapper in his suit and waistcoat. He sent Kate pictures throughout the function, and all the groomsmen wore superman socks, which was really cute! Kate woke up the next morning to a picture of Liam's message from his fortune cookie that he had opened, "the Best is yet to come". Kate had the biggest smile on her face! Wow, indeed, this was a great message, and a phrase that summed up what Kate had been experiencing in her newfound freedom.

Liam really wanted to see Kate on the day that he returned after his friend's wedding. Dick, however, used to visit the house every Saturday, and he would sit around the entire day until evening. How ironic, Dick preferred sitting at his ex-wife's house rather than with his mother! Kate could understand that she was surely driving him nuts! Kate was also keen to see Liam, and wanted to kiss him for the first time! So, she agreed that she would wait for Dick to leave and let Liam know when it was safe for him to come over. Kate suggested a chilled pizza and wine evening. Kate was done having to hide and make arrangements to meet Liam, and did not see the problem with him coming to see her at home. Kate believed she was an adult, and she did not see why she needed to be putting her life on hold because of Dick. Murphy's Law would be that Dick decided to cut the lawn and chat to the neighbours and left later than usual on this Saturday, but this didn't matter as Liam was eagerly awaiting her message to get in his car and drive to Kate.

Kate and Liam were chatting on WhatsApp whilst waiting for Dick to leave. Liam's sister was visiting South Africa at the time. His sister married a Chinese gentleman and was living in China. He had shown his mum and sister pictures of Kate, and they were both happy for him if he was happy. Kate was quite surprised that Liam also shared with them that she was older than him, divorced, and of a different race!

Dick finally left, and Kate messaged Liam to let him know that the coast was clear. Kate was really excited again, and it was the first time that Liam was going to meet Titus and Leah. He loved dogs as well! Liam arrived, and Kate was not the only excited one ... Titus and Leah went crazy! Titus was jumping around, and even dropped Kate's painting that had not been framed yet and was sitting on a ledge in the kitchen. Kate offered Liam something to drink once they all settled down. Then she gave him a tour of the house.

They ordered pizza, and Kate had the TV on with music playing in the background. They never ran out of things to talk about, and it was always so comfortable when they were together. After they ate, they decided to chill in the cinema room.

Liam seemed quite nervous as they were both anticipating their first kiss having chatted about it on many occasions before. For some reason, Kate decided to take his hand first which was quite out of character for her! His skin felt good, and it was awesome just holding hands. His touch made Kate weak at the knees. Not long after, Liam leaned in and kissed Kate. She was completely swept off her feet; it felt amazing, so gentle, soft and sweet. Kate had never been kissed like that before, and she had not felt such amazing sensations before! They had many sessions of kissing, and each time just felt even better than the previous! They would stop, have a break, have a little giggle, and then continue!

Kate needed to go and fetch her lip moisturiser, which happened to be in her bedroom. Liam spontaneously decided to lift her up and see how heavy she was, and then proceeded to carry her to her bedroom. Kate was literally lifted off her feet this time, and she completely felt like a queen! Dick had only carried her like that on their wedding night, and she believed it was more to do with her being drunk as opposed to him really wanting to carry her over the wedding threshold!

Kate was completely blown away, and the butterflies were most definitely there!!! Liam and Kate's first kiss exceeded all her expectations, and she was glad that it felt great for him as well! Time just flew by and before they knew, it was the early hours of the morning and he needed to leave.

The next day Liam had to pack and prepare for his trip to the UK for the week. He called Kate from the airport before he left and sent a message in the morning once he arrived. Their chats decreased in the week due to the time difference and Liam being out and about. Kate and Liam were already in a routine of speaking to each other every night. On the second last night, Liam broke the news to Kate that there was an offer for him to go and work in the UK office. Kate's heart sank; she could not believe that they were just falling for each other, and there was a possibility that he would have to leave. He could sense the anxiety on her end, but nothing was confirmed. So, they were going to wait and see. On Liam's last day in the UK, he had almost an entire day before his flight back home that evening. He did some walking around London, but always went back to the vicinity of his office just so that he would have a Wi-Fi connection to talk to Kate! Kate was smitten by Liam's investment in time!

Liam arrived back the following day and was completely exhausted. His sister and her husband were still in town, and they were all celebrating Chinese New Year that day. So, there was no chance for Kate and Liam to see each other.

Liam was a real gentleman! Besides them both taking things at a pace that was comfortable for both, it took Liam over a month before he started to open up and share how he felt about the physical attraction and chemistry that existed between them.

Kate left the following morning for her first work trip to Kenya. Kate and Liam were in contact throughout, and had much fun in the evenings when she was back in her hotel room. They had great chemistry and good creativity which kept their imaginations going whilst apart. The conversations whilst Kate was in Kenya were the spark for what was still to come!

Kate returned from her trip, and that weekend was Valentine's Day. Before she arrived back, Liam asked if she had plans for the day, and suggested they go for lunch and spend the day together. They started looking for options of where to go and, since they both loved Italian cuisine, they chose an Italian restaurant called Cornuti. It was ironic as the meaning of Cornuti translates to "horns," and in their naughty conversations with each other they would always use the purple smiley emoji with the horns!

Kate started to wonder what gift she should get Liam. She did not want to go over the top as it was still early on in their relationship, but at the same time, she really wanted to get him something. She brought back coffee from Kenya, and since Liam was a fan of *Happy Socks,* she decided to get him two pairs of those.

In the build-up to Valentine's Day, Liam insisted he would fetch Kate and drive her to lunch. Again, an action of a real gentleman! Kate really felt it was out of his way as he was passing the restaurant, then driving to her, and then they would have to drive back in the direction he had just come from. But eventually she decided it was a kind gesture and accepted.

Kate was nervous and excited in the build-up to him arriving. She could not believe that she had a date on Valentine's Day! When Liam arrived, he greeted her and said that she looked really nice. It was extremely hot, easily around 32°C. Kate chose to wear a cool, flowing long dress with thin straps. Liam came in and greeted the dogs, and once they put them away, they left to lunch.

Lunch was pleasant and enjoyable, with great food. They decided not to have dessert, as Kate had many delectable treats waiting for them at home. The day before, she went out and bought a few of their favourite snacks, like cheeses, olives, spreads, fruit, champagne and dessert!

It was an absolute scorcher of a day, in all senses! Liam always wore sneakers, and Kate had to convince him to dip his feet in the swimming pool with her to cool down a bit. They had many giggles around his skin complexion in contrast to hers! Yes, Liam was Caucasian indeed, but really on the lighter spectrum, and next to her milk chocolate complexion, it was exceptionally contrasting! Whilst it did not bother either of them, they just drew in the experience as they held hands and touched each other's feet whilst submerged under the water.

There was of course lots of kissing, talking and laughter. Before Kate knew it, they were both on the couch and Liam began undoing her dress. It felt good, all the touching, caressing, kissing and embracing! Liam was gentle and undemanding, whilst still being extremely charismatic. His approach was comforting given that this would be her first time sharing with someone intimately other than Dick. In her mind in the build-up and anticipation of this moment, there was a particular song that she really liked that was released in the previous year. The lyrics were very fitting once Kate had met Liam and realised the spark and chemistry that existed between them. Kate told him that she wanted this song to play in the background! The name of the song is "Firestone", by Kygo.

Kate and Liam were both very nervous, but expectedly so, as this was the first time for both after being in long term, serious relationships. Once the deed was done, Liam said, "I bet you were not expecting that to have happened so soon"! Well indeed, they were both not expecting it that soon, but as they had agreed before, if they were both comfortable in the moment, it was good to go!

However, Kate did analyze the experience repeatedly in her head thereafter. Her biggest concern was that she did not climax; however, this was understandable as it was her first time with someone new.

Kate and Liam connected on many different levels, conversation was never a problem, and they never ran out of things to talk about. The interaction was always pleasant and comfortable. Often when they would chat on WhatsApp, they would say the same things and were completely aligned in terms of thought processes. Kate really enjoyed talking to Liam, and he became her go-to person. He was the first person that she would message about anything, and she often used him as a sounding board when it came to Dick and his actions. Kate enjoyed the freedom of not having to answer to someone for everything. Liam never criticised her, and she was completely carefree.

Liam was blown away with the first meal that Kate prepared for them. His ex-girlfriend only cooked for him once and, on that occasion, she used mince that had gone bad! He was ill for a week thereafter! He could not believe the effort that Kate had taken in preparing a three-course meal, including a homemade vanilla Panna Cotta with a mixed berry coulis. Kate had a special bottle of red wine that she had received as a gift, and she had been waiting for a special occasion since 2013 to open it. Kate had decided that this was the perfect night and time to crack open the bottle! Liam loved all the food, and the wine too! He said that no one had ever cooked like that for him besides his mom!

Kate had many first experiences that were shared with Liam. When they were not with each other, Kate and Liam had many fun-filled and pleasurable hours sexting, and there were many exchanges of nudes and raunchy photos. Liam boosted Kate's self-confidence, and as she got more comfortable in her own skin, together with her drive for creativity, the manifestations and possibilities were limitless!

Kate's next business trip was in early March to the UK. She was fortunate to have some additional free time to spend with her family. When she got back on the Saturday, Kate went to a gin and tonic festival with Rebecca. The following day, Liam was going over to spend the day with her. Kate was excited as she had not seen him for two weeks. Just as he left to drive out to see her, his car tyre started giving him trouble and he had to turn back. Whilst Kate was disappointed, she was also grateful that his tyre did not burst, and he was safe.

Later that evening, Liam said he needed to chat with Kate and had hoped that he could have done it in person as was planned, but this was not the case. He felt that things were going too fast between them and that they were getting too serious, and there was a very good possibility that he was going to take the job offer in the UK.

Kate was really saddened by the news and frustrated. She did not understand it, as they both decided on the pace of their relationship, and clearly did not expect that they were both going to fall for each other that soon! She agreed to give him some space to think things over. After two weeks with minimal chatting between, they agreed to meet.

Liam went over, and they had a discussion. It was so different to what Kate was used to with Dick, because her opinion counted! He explained how he felt and asked her what her thoughts were. In her mind, he was not going to be leaving the following day neither did he have a date confirmed; it was just a possibility. Kate asked him if he enjoyed the time they spent together, and if there were any other concerns between them. She suggested that if he was still happy, they could continue as they were doing, and they could cross the bridge of him leaving when it actually happened. He confirmed that he really enjoyed spending time with her, and he liked her mature outlook, which made a lot of sense. Therefore, their relationship continued!

As time passed, Kate and Liam shared more intimately. They were comfortable with each other and orgasming for Kate was not an issue. They would take a bubble bath together, massage each other and just soak up what each person had to offer. The first time they took a bubble bath reminded Liam of his ex, and he mentioned it had been a long time since he had done that with someone. Kate never imagined that she would enjoy having sex as much as she did! In one day, they could easily go for three to four rounds! Every time they met, they would have different positions that they wanted to try and experiment with. There were many rooms in the house that they had many sensual experiences in, but the most favourite was always the bedroom with the mirrors! Liam was fascinated with Kate's physique, and he would always comment on how amazingly sexy her body was.

Kate's experiences with Liam were remarkable! Every time he just kissed her or touched her, she would go weak at the knees. This was what she had imagined her first time would have been like. The song that comes to mind is Madonna's "Like a Virgin". Liam most certainly loved Kate back to life, gave her a newfound confidence and allowed her to openly share and experience intimacy like never before.

Liam shared with his best mate what an amazing and kind person Kate was (not to forget an excellent chef as well!). He always commended her kindness and said that he knew very few people as kind as Kate. He also asked Kate to bear with him in terms of him taking things slow, and freaking out now and again. He explained that in his previous relationship, things had gone really fast too, and, in the end, it didn't work out the way he wanted. That's why this time around, he wanted to do things differently. Kate was okay with the pace at which they were going; it was just the exclusivity of their relationship that was important to her.

CHAPTER 14
Titanium-Strong

Dick met a few of Kate's friends at a comedy show, and mentioned to them that he was so happy that Kate had moved on and met someone. Her friends were completely surprised and shocked, and came back to tell Kate that she should be careful who she was speaking to, as someone had told Dick that she was seeing Liam. Kate realised that the only person that could have told him was Maria. She knew it would not have been intentional, and Maria would not have realised what the possible consequences of her actions would have been.

Not long after this, the first draft of the divorce settlement agreement was sent to Dick for review. He immediately messaged Kate and wanted to discuss if they could keep their pension and retirement funds separately. Kate did not want to get into an argument with him. This was not included in their anti-nuptial agreement and therefore, legally, the monies had to be added together and split 50-50. Kate suggested that it should rather be discussed through their lawyers. Dick got extremely upset with her, and this was when the tables started to change.

Kate's next business trip was to Germany. Prior to her leaving, Dick contacted their German friends. Kate found this very strange, as initially he did not bother to contact them to tell them about the divorce, but now felt the need to say something because he knew she was going to be spending time with them. Kate had an amazing trip to Germany. It was the first time that she got to meet her new boss in person, and he was such an awesome guy! She also got to spend quite a bit of personal time with their German friends. Kate had decided that she wanted to taste beer and thought no better place to do it than in Germany. The 16th April would have been Kate and Dick's 10th wedding anniversary. Thankfully, Kate was with good supportive friends on that day and far away from home. Whilst Kate did not want to be with Dick anymore, it was still a significant milestone, and the mind wonders about how it all could have panned out differently. Just a few months prior, Kate was picking out her white wedding dress in preparation for their anniversary as Dick promised that they could renew their vows in the Maldives, and Kate could then get to wear the white dress which she always dreamt of.

Liam was extremely supportive and could pick up over the phone from so far away that Kate was struggling. It really meant a lot to her that they were connected, and he knew when she required words of encouragement.

The following day, Kate returned home to South Africa. When she got to the airport, she called Maria to wish her for her birthday! She sounded very concerned, and frantically explained to Kate that it looked like Dick had moved back into the house! He had a lot of clothes and belongings back in the house. Kate was under the impression that he had just brought a lot of his personal things over the two-week period, and he was probably still going to return that evening to collect all his stuff.

When Kate got back home, Maria told her that Dick had a braai with his family the previous day. The house was a complete mess! Kate felt violated! Whilst part of the house still belonged to Dick on paper, this was now her private space! She could not believe that his family did not have a problem coming into her space to enjoy a braai together. Did they not have any other venue where this could have been done?! His mother did not even have the decency to send Kate a message, but was now quite content to be enjoying family time in her private space. Kate looked through the bedrooms, and Maria was indeed correct, all of Dick's clothes were back and items such as his golf clubs were even back! This looked like a permanent move back!

Dick arrived later that evening from work, barely greeted Kate and then asked if she wanted dinner because he was going out to buy Maria Chicken Licken! Kate asked him what he meant by this, and he casually confirmed that he had moved back in because this was his house and dogs too, and the divorce process was taking way too long! Kate asked him why he did not consult with her, and he said that she told him she did not want to discuss anything!

Kate decided not to discuss anything further with him. Her body and mind were in turmoil! The only thing that she had said to him was that they should communicate via their lawyers when it came to the settlement agreement and the calculation of who gets what. This was the reason why they had lawyers, to ensure that the process was fairly completed, and to prevent them from arguing. Kate felt it was extremely childish of him to just move back in after being out of the house for more than six months already! This was her private space; how dare he just decide on his own that he would move back in. She was frantic and did not know what to do. It was around 19:00 and Kate decided to call her lawyer to ask for advice.

Her lawyer explained that legally Dick still owned fifty percent of the house, and it was probably best that they draft a letter in the morning to Dick and formally send him their position. Kate made herself something to eat, took the dogs, and went and locked herself up in her bedroom. She could not believe the move that Dick had just made!

The next morning, Kate's lawyer sent Dick the letter explaining to him that he had chosen to leave the matrimonial residence six months prior and already had alternative accommodation at his mother, and they requested that he moved out on the day of the receipt of the letter. They also mentioned that Kate was kind enough to allow Dick to stay at the house whilst she was away on her business trip. They highlighted the issues of domestic violence, which could occur with him relocating, and the fact that Kate did not trust him and felt unsafe with him being in her space. Her lawyer advised her against any application of the use of the Domestic Violence Act, on the assumption that Dick would move out on the day that the notification was received. Within two hours of sending the notification, they received a response from his lawyer saying that Dick would come and collect his things that evening.

Kate felt really awful that things had to go this way, but she did not believe that it was fair that Dick invaded her space without even consulting her, and given such a long time period had elapsed after him initially moving out. He had chosen to move out, how could he just choose when he wanted to come back into her space? Kate felt that Dick did whatever he wanted to, whenever he wanted to. Her feelings or existence was never considered; it was always about him. That evening Dick arrived in a sullen mood and took all his belongings.

Two days later, Kate's lawyer had to send the updated agreement with requested changes. In response to this draft, her lawyer received a response from Dick's lawyer that took Kate completely by surprise!

Dick stated that Titus was his dog and, as such, he would be taking him away when he moved out from his mother's place at the beginning of June. Kate could not believe this; Dick had agreed that both dogs would not be split and would remain with her! He was even willing to pay maintenance toward them, as he said they were like his kids.

Kate was in a complete turmoil when she read the email. She was angry and upset, and could not believe that Dick would go to this extreme and unsettle the dogs!

Two months prior, Kate had consulted with a dog behaviourist. Titus was an extremely nervous and timid dog, and Kate believed that he had gone through many significant life changes in a short space of time. He had recently swallowed her gym sock, started to destroy a pair of her shoes and was just, in general, anxious. Any slight change to his routine affected him!

The behaviourist came over to the house and did an assessment focusing on Titus, and in addition, observing the interaction and relationship with Leah. Dick wanted to attend the session, but Kate felt that it would just cause more confusion as he no longer lived with them. It made more sense for Maria and her to attend the session alone. The behaviourist shared simple ideas and different ways to manage the two dogs. She empathised with Kate, highlighting that she literally had a teenage dog that had struggled with the formative time period until adolescence, was exposed to many adverse life changes, had to deal with the introduction of Leah, and then lastly Dick leaving home.

The behaviourist could not definitely say what would be better for the two dogs, but did observe an extremely close attachment or bond between Titus and Leah. Kate shared the report and all of the learnings with Dick.

Therefore, it made sense in their response to Dick's request to share that it would be in the best interest of both dogs to keep them together, as an extremely strong bond had been formed between them. Furthermore, they believed that Dick was simply using Titus as a tool to manipulate Kate, given that he had previously stated that the two dogs would remain together and under her care when he left the matrimonial home in October 2015. Kate decided to give up on all of the monetary battles which included Dick wanting her off his medical insurance by the beginning of June, him wanting all of the expenses to be split into two, requiring her to pay for fifty percent of everything (although their earnings were not of the same ratio), seeing to her own lawyer's account and him taking the majority of their assets/furniture all in the hope that she could keep Titus with her.

Dick's response was that he was willing to exchange Titus for Leah, but both dogs were no longer going to remain with her. He also wanted an additional clause stating that neither of them was allowed to transfer ownership of their dog to a third party without providing the first option to the owner of the other dog. He also used the behaviourist to his advantage by contacting her and asking her to write a letter of recommendation. In this letter, she stated that there is no accurate decision as to which dog should be re-homed, and the repercussions of which would be unknown until four to six weeks after the change, and reassessing the anxiety and stress associated with the change. She also mentioned that, given the dogs were seven months apart in age, this had them potentially over-bonding and developing various fear-based behaviours. Whilst it was not a rule, it was, however, often a known repercussion amongst puppies growing together. Therefore, in her professional opinion, she believed that there may be an advantage of separating the dogs in order to prevent potential problems later on as they grew, developed and matured.

Kate could not comprehend how tactless Dick was, offering her to choose between the two dogs. Whilst Titus and her had a very special bond indeed, Leah and Titus both were her children, and she could not choose the one over the other! Did Dick honestly think this was a game? Kate's lawyer advised that Kate meet him over coffee to try to discuss the matter.

Kate used the next opportunity of Dick going over to the house as her chance to ask him why he was behaving in this manner – he had agreed to not separate the dogs and to leave them in her care. Kate argued that if Dick really cared about them in the way that he claimed, he would not be doing this. Dick laughed at Kate in a sinister tone and said that he could not talk to her, and she should speak to his lawyer! Kate was fuming and enraged and felt sick within!

In the days to come, Kate felt extreme pain and hurt. She chatted to her lawyer, and he explained that dogs were not considered children, and it would cost her a large sum of money to fight for the dogs to remain together.

Kate found herself wedged in a corner. When thinking about the situation in an empathetic manner, she reasoned with herself, convincing herself that perhaps Dick required this unconditional love from the companionship of Titus. He was all alone without a supportive network of family and friends, like she was fortunate to have. At the end of the day, Dick chose, and he selected Titus, irrespective of the bond that she had with Titus, or the significance of the role that he played in her life. Dick had chosen him, and thus had ownership of him on paper. It still irked her, though, that he had not been with Titus since October when he left home, but now decided he wanted him! Kate also decided not to be so hard on herself in terms of how she could rescue or change the circumstances that she was being faced with. Dick was making the choice to split the dogs, and it was on his terms. Her heart would be broken because of the separation from Titus, and the separation of Titus from Leah.

Kate responded to her lawyer and agreed that Dick could keep Titus, and she would keep Leah. There was no other dispute, and the paperwork could be finalised.

In the meantime, excitement continued as the building of Liam's apartment drew to completion. Kate was thrilled that Liam would soon be living very close to her, and would not have very far to travel in the future! In anticipation of his new home, and thoughts of what gift to get him, she asked him for his favourite landscape photo. Kate wanted to do a canvas painting for him but due to time constraints, she had the photo printed on canvas for him. She also bought him a bottle of champagne to honour this significant milestone in his life. Liam was due to collect the keys to his new apartment whilst his parents were away in China to witness the arrival of his niece! Kate suggested that they go out and celebrate this special occasion! So, they arranged to meet at the apartment so he could show her the place, and then they went out for dinner.

Liam was blown away with the gift and champagne and kept telling Kate that he did not deserve all of this!

On Friday the 27th May, the final papers were ready, and Kate's lawyer brought them to her so they could sign them and get them to Dick as soon as possible. Kate's reaction was nothing like she expected. She had imagined a huge celebration, but instead she cried the entire morning after signing the papers. She could not stop the tears from flowing. Eventually, Kate left work by lunchtime and made an appointment to do her nails to try to lift her spirits. When she got home, she decided to have an afternoon nap as she felt emotionally drained. She was not sad about the outcome, but rather it was now a reality that the final steps had been taken for the finalisation of the divorce.

The following day, Kate felt much better, and it was her cousin's wife's birthday. It was the perfect opportunity to celebrate with her family. They went out for dinner and dancing, and Kate had great fun! It was just what she needed to lift her energy and mood.

Dick notified Kate that he had found a place of his own to rent and would be collecting the furniture, all of his belongings and Titus on the 2nd June.

Kate felt miserable in the days leading up, as she thought of Leah, Maria and her parting with Titus. Dick did not make it any easier. He literally shopped around their house and asked Kate to split their linen, towels and whatever he could take with him to set up his new place! He was of the opinion that Kate should have been grateful that he was leaving her entire kitchen, and only asked for old drinking glasses and coffee mugs that he knew she was not using. Kate felt as though Dick was literally extracting life out of her. It was not as though he could not afford to buy himself the miscellaneous items he required.

Kate was grateful and extremely fortunate to be away on a business trip to Cape Town on the day that Dick came to collect everything and her baby Titus.

Her biggest concern was that she was letting Titus down and not keeping to the promise that she made him. She always told him when Dick had left home that she would never leave him, she would always be with him, and that he had nothing to worry about. With a broken heart, her story changed, reassuring Titus that she had no choice and that Dick wanted him to stay with him rather than with Leah and her.

That morning Kate said goodbye to her baby, the one that brought her so much unconditional love, the one that remained loyal to her, the one that filled her heart with happiness and fulfilment. She did not know whether she would ever see him again. How could life be so cruel? Her heart felt immense pain and ached knowing that evening when she returned home, Titus would not be there to greet her.

Leah and Kate struggled in the days to come. It was the start of winter, which ironically summed up their moods and feelings of emptiness and detachment. Leah did not eat anything for about five full days, and walked around the house with her head down, lost and no verve in her body.

On the Saturday after Titus left, Liam had plans to go to a music concert with his mates and had no plans of seeing Kate on the Sunday. Kate called Liam that Saturday afternoon as she and Leah sat on the couch, depressed. He did not take her call, but later Kate saw that he was online on WhatsApp. Therefore, he blatantly ignored her. Two weeks prior to this, he did the same thing but apologised profusely. He said it was very wrong of him to do this, and he knows what it feels like, as it had been done to him before. That evening when he got home, he did not send Kate a message either. It was routine between them to let each other know when either of them was home safely after a night out.

The next morning, Liam greeted Kate as normal. When she enquired about why he had ignored her, he said she was making assumptions. He decided immediately that he no longer wanted to be in a relationship! He said that this issue was happening far too often between them, and that he decided this was not for him! Once again, someone else decided for Kate that the relationship was over!

Kate and Liam chatted for a bit, but he had made up his mind, thanked her for the great times they shared and said they will always be friends!

Kate was shattered and heartbroken ... Every inch of her heart, head, body and soul ached.

CHAPTER 15
Resilience

Kate's lawyer advised her that it would not take very long to get the summons for the divorce issued, and a court date, if Dick and his lawyer had done their part correctly post the signing of the settlement agreement. Kate followed up with Dick and, of course, there were delays even though everything on their end was done to speed up the process.

On the 23rd June, Kate's lawyer received details from Dick's lawyer, stating she could contact the sheriff in the meantime to arrange a suitable time for him to call on her or, alternatively, attend the sheriff's office and have them serve the summons on her.

They agreed that it would be best for Kate to go and collect the summons. Rebecca advised Kate to take a friend with or her mum for moral support, as it is also an emotional part of the process. Kate decided to take Jade with her. Jade worked with Kate, and had been her pillar of strength when Liam decided to leave. Every day, Kate shared her feelings, fears and thoughts with her.

Kate received details of the address of the Sherriff's office. She was somewhat nervous, as she did not know what to expect, but at the same time rather pleased that she was another step closer to being legally divorced. When they arrived at the office, Jade and Kate were met by Mari at reception, who did not even greet them. Kate then proceeded to explain the reason she was there and quoted the case number issued to her by her lawyer. When Mari entered the number into the system, she could not pick up the case. Kate started repeating the number, and Mari sarcastically said to Kate that she was not working there from yesterday and she knew her case number. The case number did not exist and could not be found!

Mari was extremely rude and gave Kate a lot of attitude. She belittled her, saying, "So it is a divorce and you the defendant," loud enough for everyone around to hear, and in a very condescending tone. Kate then gave her Dick's lawyer's number. She had numerous issues with the telephone lines and eventually got through. Mari spoke to the lawyer's secretary in Afrikaans as if Kate could not understand and said that Kate was already not impressed with her.

It was a new and unpleasant situation for Kate, and Mari did not help making it any easier.

Kate eventually went up to the deputy Sherriff where she was to sign and accept the summons. She asked Kate whether she wanted to contest the divorce or was willing to accept it. Kate was surprised that there was still a period after the signing of the settlement agreement that one could change your mind. Well, after all she had been through there was only one way forward for her! Kate was happy and confident to sign!

Kate laid a complaint about Mari's poor attitude. The Sheriff got Mari to call with the intention of apologizing to Kate. However, instead Mari asked Kate why she had reported her to her boss even though she went through all the trouble to assist her, and said Kate needed to accept the apology. Mari eventually hung up on Kate.

Mari really lacked any empathy and did not make Kate's challenging day any easier. However, Kate was relieved that she was a step further to the divorce being concluded and closed out.

It was at this time that Kate decided to put her power of manifestation into play. She decided to shop around for a new apartment in preparation for when the house would be sold. The house had been on the market for about eighteen months, and they had not received any written offers. Kate started looking at property online and was keen to look at new developments, as this would give her sufficient time to sell the house. Kate stumbled upon a gem that was perfect for Leah and her. The location, the space, the layout and design of the property was exactly what Kate wanted, and so she decided to put in an offer to purchase. The completion of the building was only expected to be completed in five to six months' time, and Kate really believed that the house would be sold by then. The offer to purchase was subject to the sale of the current house.

In the meantime, Kate put all of her energy into this new home and space that was soon to be hers. She started shopping around for a few new items of furniture, would make time once a week to take a drive and view the progress on the construction, and often daydreamed of Leah and her in this new home. Kate was excited about the new space and being able to make choices and decisions independently.

Dick sent Kate a message to inform her that the court date was set for the 1st September. Thankfully, Kate did not need to go to court, but Dick had to attend in person. Her lawyer explained to her that depending on the capacity of the Judge, the decree could be issued immediately, or it could take a few weeks after for it to be issued.

Spring day had never been significant to Kate but, on this morning, she awoke really feeling the new beginning that lay ahead. Being the empath that she was, she also spent much time thinking of Dick and how he was feeling having to stand in front of the Judge and state why he wanted this divorce. Whilst it was a simple standard statement and routine practice, Kate could not help but feel for him. As a result, Kate did not follow-up with him or check how things went or if the decree was issued. She also did not hear from Dick at all. Two days later after chatting to a friend, who asked how it went, Kate decided to send Dick a message. This was a huge milestone in her life, and she deserved to know if it was all well concluded. Kate was driving to an art class in Pretoria that morning and cried her heart out when Dick's response came through. He casually confirmed that the decree was immediately issued on 1st September, and the divorce had been finalised.

A wave of emotions ran through Kate – she felt hurt, pain, immense sadness, anger and relief. She was not unhappy with the outcome, but it was a reality! Kate was officially divorced on paper and in the eyes of the law. She could not believe that Dick did not bother to tell her that he got the decree on the day. She was extremely emotional over the next few days, and it did not take much for her to start crying. It was the final emotional release of the relationship officially ending.

Kate decided to reach out to Liam first after the break-up to demonstrate her maturity and to ask how he was and what was happening in his life. He responded, but she could gather that he was still in the same position as before when it came to settling down. Whilst she knew where she stood with him, there was always a little hope that maybe something would change. Kate was on a low, and it seemed as though not much was going her way.

In the weeks to come, Kate became extremely focused on selling the house and pushing to move onto her next chapter. She spent a lot of time planning and envisaging how she would decorate her new apartment. She eventually even started shopping around for new items to furnish her new apartment! Every Sunday was a show day, and the pressure was on to sell the house. Kate would follow-up with the agents all the time and made sure that everyone was playing their part to get the house sold so that she could move into her new place.

Kate went to the property attorney's office to sign the final papers a month before the planned occupation date of her new apartment. Kate was almost certain that she was sent an angel that day. She was extremely anxious, and she required a bit more than a miracle. There was a month to go, and she still had no offer to purchase on her house yet! Although her end of the agreement had not yet been fulfilled in that the deal was subject to the sale of her house, the consultant was so motivating and spoke as if a miracle was still to happen. Not for a moment did any negative thought cross her mind. This place was hers no matter what!

Every second day thereafter, secretaries would call from the attorney enquiring if the house had been sold. Kate felt as though she could not breathe. She wanted to move into this new place so desperately, yet nothing was in her control. Three weeks later the inevitable occurred, Kate received a call from the attorney stating that the deal was no longer as she had not fulfilled the requirements of the agreement.

Her heart shattered and ached! She could not believe that she was once again faced with disappointment and heartache. It seemed so unfair that Dick had moved on, and he was in a financial position to cover half the expenses for the house and rent a new apartment. Kate could not help but feel like the victim in this situation. She was accepting of everything, the divorce and the new direction, but why was it not just simple to physically move on – was this too much to ask for? After a few minutes of intense crying and release, it was time again to pick herself up and continue with the present.

Kate had planned on setting up herself in her new place during the December holidays, and she was therefore dreading the free time coming up.

CHAPTER 16
Let Us Fly

It was in the middle of January that Kate decided to start private art classes. On the first day that she met the art teacher, there was an immediate physical attraction. He exemplified the kind of significant other that she would imagine herself to be partnered with. He was tall, had blonde hair, had a chiselled, naturally-tanned body, and the most amazing, unfathomable, deep, glistening-blue eyes. Kate had never seen such magnificent eyes before!

Matt had her mobile number, and initial contact made with Kate was around her signing up to the class. After her first lesson, Matt would check in to see how she was progressing with her homework and review the work that needed to be covered before the next lesson. Matt was extremely friendly and had a very warm energy and disposition. Kate's instinct told her that perhaps he was just this way with her because she was a new client, and he was making sure that she was content with the service being rendered!

It did not take long before the conversation ventured outside of art and the reason for them meeting. Matt and Kate began chatting about life. He asked Kate how long she had been divorced, and what were the reasons for the split. In the days to follow, they spent much time getting to know each other. Kate enjoyed chatting to him and seeing him twice a week for her lessons. There was a sense of familiarity and feeling at ease when she was around him. Conversation continued to become routine, and they spent considerable time in the evenings chatting. Matt openly complimented Kate, and was not shy at all. He shared what his thoughts were about her looks and physique. For some reason whilst Kate found his behaviour to be quite flattering, she did not just jump in, reciprocate or let on that she too had similar feelings about him. Kate did, however, begin to feel as though there was something more to this connection, other than the physical attraction between them.

Kate decided to do some homework to see if she could gain more insight, and so she searched through Matt's social media profiles. There was no indication of any relationship status, and all his photos and tags included group photos of friends both males and females. This confirmed the signs that she was observing, and that the feeling of excitement was genuinely accurate.

During a normal conversation, Kate asked Matt what he was doing the one Saturday afternoon, and he proceeded to tell her that he was chilling with Fluff! It sounded like a puppy to Kate, so she continued to ask who Fluff was?! Matt went on to calmly say... it was his girlfriend! That was his nickname for her...and he thought Kate knew that he had a girlfriend from Facebook.

Kate was so angry! She could not believe this! She had indeed checked out his social media profiles but, as mentioned, there was no indication from statuses, posts or pictures that Matt was in a relationship! Never mind the fact that he had been spending the prior couple of weeks openly flirting with her, complimenting her and chatting to her for hours at a time. How could he be in a relationship, but also be on his phone all the time with her, at night and over the weekends too! Moreover, he never mentioned his girlfriend at all to Kate! What on earth did she miss!

Kate told him that she did not realise that he was in a relationship! He also apologised and defended himself by confessing that he would often find himself in such trouble due to his friendly nature! Kate was extremely angry with herself, and she felt seriously misled by him! She did not have the strength to get into a discussion with him around the fact that his social media profiles and status, never mind his behaviour and actions toward her, were deceitful. Kate decided to just let it go but did mention to him that they had to stop their conversations as she did not want to get into any trouble now that she was aware that he was in a relationship. Matt still felt that there was no harm in them talking and having each other in their lives, and did not acknowledge that his behaviour and feelings shared were not appropriate given that he was in a relationship.

Kate decided to take some time out and reflect. It was early days into her classes that she had started with him, and she needed to decide whether she was going to ask the academy for a new teacher or continue with Matt.

Kate could not believe that she had fallen for Matt and his deception! She was angry with herself and needed to work on forgiving herself. She kept trying to understand why Matt had come into her life. What was she meant to learn from this experience? At this stage, Kate had no answers. However, given her kind nature, she decided to give Matt a second chance to continue being her art teacher, and so she forgave him. Kate did not discuss the issue again with him but refrained from spending time outside of their classes chatting to him.

The first class after discovering that Matt had a girlfriend was awkward initially, but thereafter he continued as normal, and they got on with their project. Kate kept wishing that she did not have insight into his true feelings for her because deep down she really liked him and felt a strong attraction toward him. It made it difficult to ignore this and continue, but it had to be done given that he was in a relationship.

Weeks continued, and Matt would take the odd opportunity to still flirt. When they got onto the topic of relationships, he decided again to share that if he were not in a relationship with Fluff, he would want to get involved with Kate. Again, whilst this was flattering, what was Kate meant to do with the information?! Matt also started to share a lot about their relationship. Early on, he did not say much but later felt comfortable to tell Kate what their challenges were. It all then made sense to Kate: why he flirted with her and why he was searching outside their relationship for more.

Kate was at the studio the one day, and Fluff stopped by to drop off something for Matt. This was the first time that Kate had the opportunity to meet her. Kate felt awful as she seemed like a sweet girl, and she had no clue what had transpired, and what was going on in terms of Matt sharing his feelings toward Kate. She was a pretty girl but not the person that Kate imagined Matt to be in a relationship with. Kate was quite disappointed as she felt that they all could have been friends. Kate enjoyed making new connections with people, but this was one in which she needed to maintain her distance.

Kate met the owner of the academy on a few occasions and in chatting, they decided to set up a coffee social. Matt and his girlfriend were included, and a few other people from the studio. Matt asked Kate if he could invite his friend whom he thought she would get along well with. Not to mention that he also described this friend as being bisexual! How desperate did Matt think Kate was?

On the day of the social, Matt's friend and girlfriend arrived together with him. It was easy to see how much in love Fluff was with Matt. This girl clearly cared deeply for him! They had a good and enjoyable time, and Kate got along well with Matt's friend, but quickly identified he was another cup of tea!

Fluff and Kate became friends on social media, and she said they should hang out more often. Kate finally decided to let her in as she did not feel guilty anymore. She had not done anything wrong, and she was a nice person. Kate started to see more of Fluff and Matt in social settings outside of class, and Kate spent some time with Fluff alone. The first time that Fluff and Kate spent time alone, she opened up to Kate and shared the challenges she had in her relationship with Matt. It all started to make sense once Kate had both versions of the story. The conclusion was Matt was no longer vested in the relationship but was still staying in it because of fear of the consequence of leaving her. Fluff was extremely clingy and dependent on Matt and could not imagine herself with anyone else. Whilst they both loved and cared for each other deeply, it was not a healthy and reciprocated relationship.

Whenever Kate spent time with them, they would argue or get on each other's nerves. It was clear that they had a lot to work on. All relationships have their challenges; however, Kate could see where this was heading. It was getting quite draining to listen to both sides of the story and playing mediator between the two. Kate's connection was always stronger to Matt, but now she had opened herself to Fluff, and offered her a friendship too. Fluff was affiliated with the arts industry; she was a sculptor and often had to drive to arts affairs. She wanted Matt to attend events with her, but he had family obligations, so could not always accompany her.

One of the great parts of the attraction to Matt was his spiritual awareness, and how much alignment there was between Kate and him on this. He shared a great deal of knowledge when it came to spirituality, questions that many of us stumble upon through life's journey. Kate was amazed at how he knew all of this when she had only just become in touch with her spirituality in recent years since splitting from Dick.

Kate had asked the Creator to allow her to meet and connect with people of like-mindedness and of the same or higher vibration to her for her to learn and grow. She believed this was the reason why Matt had come into her life. She appreciated their deep conversations the most.

As time elapsed, Matt started to exercise a special gift that he had. This was his ability to connect with a person's energy, noticing their thoughts and emotions specifically. Kate attended a friend's birthday party and when she came home that evening, she had a fever and an upset tummy. Kate rarely got ill and was quite uncomfortable that evening and did not get a good night's sleep. Matt messaged her during the night asking if she was ok. Kate only responded the next morning saying she was fine. However, he asked again if she was sure she was okay as he picked up that she was not feeling well. Kate was taken aback, as no one had been so in tune with her before.

Matt and Kate had a lot in common, especially their love for art. They were both closely following a local South African Artist, and they loved her work! Kate saw an advert on Facebook for her upcoming exhibition, and she thought it would be great if a group of their friends could go along and support her work. On the day of the exhibition, Matt confirmed that morning that Fluff was ill and could no longer join them for the exhibition that evening. Kate had been looking forward to this exhibition all week and the only available people to go were Matt and her. She did not know if Matt was going to join her or not, or how Fluff would feel if she knew Matt and Kate were attending the exhibition on their own. Kate messaged Matt to ask him what the plan was, and he happily confirmed that he would be sticking to the original plan and joining Kate. He said that Fluff had no issues with him attending the exhibition alone with Kate. They agreed that they would drive together as the exhibition was far out, and they would have dinner before the event.

Later that day, Matt messaged Kate to find out what the dress code was, and things started to feel weird. It almost felt as though they were going on a date. Before Matt arrived, there was a huge thunderstorm. The drive out into the country-side was stunning; they were both enjoying the sound of Israel Kamakawiwo'ole's "Somewhere Over the Rainbow," when suddenly, a rainbow appeared in the horizon! It was a surreal moment! Matt and Kate arrived at the venue, got their tickets and went for dinner. Dinner was great. It was the first time that they were seated alone in an intimate setting, but Kate did not make too much of it. They had been through all this before; Matt was in a relationship and, therefore, nothing could happen between them. Kate and Matt were just good friends and comfortable in each other's company. Conversation flowed, and they continued to share more stories and get to know each other better. The exhibition followed, and it was amazing. They were in awe of the artist's work and her talent! When they got home, Matt continued talking to Kate in the garage and did not want to leave. He was telling her how he was not sure what mood he would find Fluff in when he got home, and he did not want to go back to that. Eventually it was late, and Fluff messaged Matt to find out where he was. He hugged Kate goodbye and left.

Once Matt started driving, he started to message Kate. He told her that someone had to tell her that she was gorgeous, and he loved spending the evening with her. Moreover, if things were different, he was still of the mindset that they stood a chance of exploring a potential relationship together. Kate thanked him for the compliment and left it at that.

A couple of weeks prior, Kate learnt from an intuitive friend that Matt and her were soul mates and that they had been in past lives together. Kate felt this was a good explanation for the magnetism that they felt toward each other, and she shared this with him.

The next morning, Matt messaged Kate to say he had forgotten something at her house and asked if he could come through to collect it. She asked if Fluff was okay with this, as she did not want her to feel insecure. He said she was fine. They got into conversation about his initial feelings, and Kate told him that she had to manage hers, as she could not share how she truly felt about him, given his relationship status. Once Kate found out that they were soul mates, it made a lot of sense to her, since it was a past life connection. They naturally would have an attraction toward each other. He then said that he could not be sure that it was just a past life connection, and that there was not a role in this lifetime. Kate immediately told him that Fluff would hate her, and she could not hurt her, as she had befriended her! Kate asked him to elaborate, and he went on to explain that he could not ignore his feelings for her. Whilst Fluff was an obstacle, he knows many people that were destined to be together that met whilst being in another relationship. In Kate's mind, whilst she knew that each relationship has its challenges, if they were meant to be together, surely there should not have been any obstacles, at least initially.. Surely, one would imagine it to be seamless and bliss from the beginning.

Matt would continue to tell Kate that he had this attraction to her in every way, and that he was in the process of analysing it. It was all new to him in this life, but it did not feel new to him in reality. He never felt this way with any of the other females he had connections with before. He felt as though he was missing something, and he felt as though Kate filled that gap. She felt like home to him. Matt was confused about it and felt that having Kate in his life either as a partner or friend would suffice; however, he needed more time to process it.

Matt came back to Kate saying that he had decided to break up with Fluff. It was a long time coming and, as a result of their meeting and the resurfacing of all these emotions, it made him come to the realisation that he needed to get out of this relationship.

The next day, Kate went in for her lesson but, to her surprise, there was no one else in the studio for a Friday evening. She also heard romantic instrumental music playing softly in the background. She called out to Matt, but there was no response. As she started to unpack her art materials, Matt appeared and told her that he had a surprise for her. He took her hand and led her to the adjacent room. In the middle of the room was the most magnificent picnic set up enclosed with many tea candles. It was absolutely beautiful! Matt said that there was just one request of her for the evening, and that was to be in the present moment, go with the flow and enjoy!

Kate and Matt always enjoyed each other's company, but the scene tonight was surely going to lead to a dangerous outcome. Matt leaned over toward Kate, and she immediately knew what was coming. She started to giggle whilst moving her head away from Matt's to avoid the inevitable of his lips meeting hers. She moved left and right and left again, and eventually he clasped his hands around her face, and they both closed their eyes and kissed each other. Their spirits felt completely free, it was something that they were both yearning for and resisting from the first time that they had met. Kate felt awful, as Matt had not completely ended it with Fluff yet, but at the same time she was so frustrated, always having to accommodate everyone else's needs over her own! Why did it have to be so complicated when in her mind it was meant to be?

Kate and Matt continued to embrace one another, and she had never felt so safe and secure as she did when she was wrapped in his arms. Kate felt completely at peace with Matt, it was something she had never felt before with anyone else, not even Liam. Time stood still as Kate and Matt looked into each other's eyes and felt the depths of each other's touch and presence. They were both floating and just could not get enough of each other. They stayed up till 4:00 that morning before finally falling asleep. Kate had never felt so content; she felt like she was completely engulfed by angel wings that surrounded her.

Kate and Matt continued to get to know one another and spend time with each other, when possible. Kate planned a holiday with a girlfriend, and before leaving, Matt and she had agreed that they would pursue a relationship, as he was wrapping things up with Fluff. Whilst Kate was away, she could feel that there was a distance between Matt and her. His WhatsApp messages were not the same, and she had this horrible feeling in her stomach that something was not aligned.

When Kate returned, Matt was extremely busy at the studio, and it seemed as though he was avoiding seeing her. It did not make sense to Kate after all the things he had shared, and he had been so persistent in pursuing a potential relationship with her.

Finally, Kate arranged to meet Matt and confronted him on his behaviour and what was going on. She also told him that if he had changed his mind about them, it was fine. He just needed to let her know so she could process the rejection and move on.

Matt began to explain to Kate that once she and him began connecting, he had a vision of a male that was soon to enter her life. This spirit had given him a clear message that in this lifetime it was not his role to be with Kate in an intimate way, and he was told to back off! He said that this man was better suited to her, and he did not believe that he was mature enough to take this a step further with her. He thanked her for awakening something inside of him that motivated him to follow his dreams. He was finally moving to Cape Town where he was to set up his own art studio.

CHAPTER 17
Metamorphosis and Virtues

Dear Readers,

My confidence had been tested once again and the important question was whether I believed I was good enough. I felt that perhaps a compatible life soulmate relationship and everlasting love were out of reach and not meant for me. I had worked so hard on the concept of self-love and genuinely believed I was making a lot of progress, but did I truly believe I was deserving of this kind of love?

As I reflect on my journey thus far, I am extremely proud of how I have evolved and ascended as a spiritual being. Looking back, there were many days and nights that I spent crying. I had been through significant emotional challenges where I was left deeply hurt and broken inside. I felt like the victim and felt sorry for myself, but one cannot spend too much time having a pity party. Life was not happening to me, and I had a choice. I explored each opportunity that was presented to me and made the decision to understand and accept what was being revealed or shown to me by the other person or the relationship. I cannot change the world or people; however, I do have the innate power to decide how I will react and respond to my experiences. After each set back or challenge, I chose to pick myself up, identify the lessons learnt, forgive myself and the other person involved and look ahead with a new inner self-discovery. Each relationship has revealed parts of myself that were unknown and has given me a deeper insight into my relationship with myself.

And so, the fire within me is reignited, nothing or no one was going to hold me back, and I continue to create and live the life that I truly desire in my heart, irrespective of my experiences.

I believe that we are powerful co-creators with the universe and the reality that we create is all resting on the choices we make. I believe in each lifetime, there are major lessons that you will experience in various relationships with specific souls that are placed on your path. However, for every decision made, the choice always remains your own. There is nothing set in stone and there are endless possibilities. I do believe that there is always a choice to be made and we are here to create and manifest the life we desire. You can achieve absolutely anything that you set your mind and heart on through the law of attraction also known as the process of manifestation, visualising and feeling into what it is that you desire and trusting that it will materialise. The answer from Creator, our source is always yes. No matter what you ask for, have faith that it will come to you with all your heart.

Obsessing and over-analysing of the potential outcome is of no benefit. One must remain present and be committed, but release the attachment to the outcome of one's desires by going with the flow and not controlling the outcomes of situations. It is a bit like planting a seed, once you have planted it, you water and nurture it, but you do not keep uprooting it to see if it is growing. The lesson learnt here is that when you connect with your heart, you become centred and aligned with your higher being, and this is where you will find flow and harmony and balance meet. It is only when you are at this point that you will experience the bliss unfold. The bliss of the asking and the reward of the receiving is all manifested in relaxation about the process, the timing of which you have no control over.

Patience and trusting are crucial in understanding that you will only ever receive what is for your highest good. This is what we sometimes find difficult to come to terms with – when one door closes, there is always other doors that open, and you will always move onto something better and more rewarding for you.

During my challenging times, the following tools have assisted in lifting my vibration:

> Always remember to breathe, we often forget this. Take the time to pause and just breathe to gain calmness within the body.

> Feel the emotions that come up and journal or write them out and burn the paper afterwards. Allow yourself to feel the various emotions which come up for you, acknowledge them and let them be. Allow yourself to cry, this is cathartic and an especially important part of the healing process. Always follow this release session with an activity that is uplifting. E.g., dancing and singing along to your favourite song, a salt bath, a comforting meal, or a walk outside in nature.

> Take accountability and acceptance of the situation, reflect on your actions and your role played in the situation or relationship. Never play the victim or blame game, one of the most rewarding actions is to take accountability, and identify what you are being taught by the situation or the person and move on from this. The person or situation is only mirroring what needs to be addressed by you and the lesson to be learnt by you.

> Nourish your body and soul by taking care of yourself; ensure you are eating healthy meals and be gentle and caring towards yourself. Positive self-talk and self-pampering is especially important too!

> Meditate daily, do a form of exercise, or even just go for a walk and be outdoors in nature.

> Ground yourself by placing your barefoot on the bare earth or imagine an energy beam of light coming up from the roots of a tree underground, through the soles of your feet and through all your chakras and out through the crown of your head.

> ➢ Carve out time every day to sit quietly with yourself, close your eyes and place your hands directly on your heart space. Feel your heartbeat and get present in your body in the now, and then ask for the guidance/clarity you are looking for. The answers lie within you, and they will come up for you. Also spend time using your imagination to dream about the type of life you wish to lead.

> ➢ Every day, take time to journal on what you are grateful for and why.

> ➢ Every day, take time to affirm into reality what you want for yourself and how you want to feel about yourself. There are many examples of affirmations out there, but you can also create your own that resonate for you. For example: I am enough, I am lovable, I am ready to receive everlasting love.

> ➢ Every day tell yourself how much you love yourself when you look at your reflection in the mirror.

> ➢ Keep your thoughts and words positive, because what you think, you create. What you feel, you attract, and what you imagine, you become.

> ➢ Have healthy boundaries in your relationships, and spend time with people that make you feel good about yourself, want only the best for you, and celebrate your successes with you!

> ➢ Spend time doing activities or hobbies that lift your spirit and make you feel good.

Based on my experiences, I have discovered that everything links to you. Always start with yourself, know who you are and what your desires are, what makes you feel happy, what makes you feel sad, and know what are the things on which you will not compromise. The only one who gets to decide your worth is you! It is called self-worth for the simple reason that it comes from you. Appreciate that you are a beautiful soul that is here on earth to love, learn, evolve and experience all that life has to offer.

By no means is self-love or self-acceptance a once-off lesson, it is a daily practice that I have been following the past six and a half years. The more you practice it, the more in alignment you find yourself, and realise that this relationship is forever changing and unfolding. My guiding gauge is that if it feels good, I am in alignment.

I continue to love myself unconditionally on my journey. I love who I am and shine my unique light and share my gifts with the world. I no longer search for love and happiness from external sources. My love and happiness come from within and any additional love and joy that I receive from my interactions with others is merely a bonus.

I am proud of who I am because I have learnt to give myself the love and acknowledgment that I deserve. Being authentic is my birthright, and everything works out in my favour as the universe co-creates with me.

I am honouring and celebrating the woman I have become because I am enough!

Yours sincerely,

Kate

Acknowledgments

A huge thank you to my wonderful friends Anastasia and Joy who constantly encouraged and believed in me. They reminded me how important it was to complete and publish this book (bearing in mind I have not had any previous experience!) as they wanted me to share my story with other women.

To my parents thank you for always supporting me no matter what choices I make in life and for always loving me no matter what! I love you both!

To all my teachers, guides, and beautiful souls that I have had the honour of interacting with on my journey, thank you all for being a part of my journey and witnessing my transformation and growth.

To Kelvin Chin, thank you for your recommendation and referral onto my incredible book manager Kathryn Bartman! Kath, thank you so much for your excellent work on managing the editing of my book and sharing your wealth of experience in self-publishing.

May you all be abundantly blessed always!